A Sho

To Andrew,

May the Rord Rise
to meet you and
may the wind be
always at your back.

Ryan Mark

Good luck in school!!

A Shot and a Prayer

By

Ryan Murphy

www.bookstandpublishing.com

Published by
Bookstand Publishing
Morgan Hill, CA 95037
3914_5

ISBN 978-1-61863-539-6
Library of Congress Control Number: 2013939020

Printed in the United States of America

Acknowledgement

This is a small story that lives within me.

My deepest gratitude goes out to my following friends:

To Tom Starita for lighting a fire within me…

To my best friend, Jon Saccenti, for encouragement and for providing a great sports angle…

To Mike Saccenti for providing quick and valuable feedback that aided my editing process…

To my wonderful mother, Jean Murphy, for helping this English teacher with his grammar

To Ann Coscio, my colleague and friend, whose finishing touches I could not do without

To KellyAnn Susino, for saving my final draft

To my students for providing inspiration

To my wife, Issela, who I lean on for true and tough love

And to my daughter, Michaela, who is the reason for everything

Without all of these people, Father Malloy and Hector are just ghosts in the pews.

To my family…

To my mom, my humble teacher

To my father, my role model

To my brother, my best man

To my wife, my true love

To my daughter, my light and my life

Chapter 1:

"My life is my message."

- *Mahatma Gandhi*

Present Day:

Staten Island Catholic Youth Organization (C.Y.O)
Championship Game!

St. Michael's vs. Our Lady of Pity

Radio Announcer:

"What a game folks! What a game! The championship hangs in the balance. Our Lady of Pity is clinging to a one point lead with just five seconds left on the clock. St. Michael's has one last shot to win the championship!"

Hector Ruiz was emotionally spent. He had been waiting for this limelight moment for years. To his amazement, all he could think about at this point were others. These thoughts revolved around his tired mother and his loving coach. Tears welled up in Hector's eyes. He knew he had to pull himself together. It all came down to one play – one play for the championship. Hector knew his team and his coach were counting on him.

5 months earlier…

"Yo, Hector, how much you got on you?" A tall, African-American teenager with a long, muscular torso shouted across the basketball court. The young man, Jamaal Jordan, was

1

sporting black and red Nike high tops, with black mesh shorts and a faded Allan Houston New York Knicks jersey.

"Fifty bucks says I take you out on the court, big man." Hector Ruiz was a cocky and loud mouthed teenager known for his quickness on the court and laziness in the classroom. It was common for the Mexican born seventeen-year-old to hustle other basketball players twice his age. Hector was not very tall, standing only 5'7 inches tall, but his speed was blinding.

The one-on-one basketball game was virtually over as soon as it started. Even though Jamaal was bigger and stronger than Hector, he could not match Hector's quickness. Hector resembled a mongoose eluding the bite of a venomous cobra as he bobbed and weaved left and right. There was nothing Jamaal could do. Jamaal knew he'd have to work an extra shift at his Shoprite gig in order to pay off his new debt.

As the two teenagers were in the twilight of their matchup, a slender, pale skinned, middle-aged man walked up to the gate at the Port Richmond High School playground. In this part of town, he stuck out like a sore thumb. Port Richmond was an urban town on the north shore of Staten Island. It consisted mostly of Mexican, Puerto Rican, and African-American families. Port Richmond was a blue collar working class town with deeply rooted family tradition. People who were born there usually grew up there, lived there and then died there. Times were, however, becoming increasingly difficult. The depressed economy put many out of work and as a result, violent gangs and neighborhood crime developed. These conditions made the neighborhood more dangerous. In this town, this stranger turned heads. The man was wearing black dress slacks with a black button-down shirt. The unusual, but pleasant-faced man completed the atypical attire by sporting a fine black blazer. In his right hand was a well-worn valise case seemingly full of clothes. Wherever this man was headed, he was going to be there for some time. There was one more unique aspect of the man in black, a white collar. He was a priest.

"What 'choo looking at white boy?" questioned Jamaal. Jamaal did not like it when people would watch him play. He didn't like it when people questioned him, judged him or criticized him. The snarl Jamaal gave the adult was one of his defense mechanisms. It usually scared off the random trouble that came his way. Undeterred, the priest looked at Jamaal and replied, "I'm looking at two strong players. If only you two refined your form, you could be special." Both Jamaal and Hector stopped playing for a moment and decided to give the stranger a go of it. "Listen man, you're mad pasty. Get out of here before I run you for your money and your Bible." The man cracked a laugh and shook his head. The man in black thanked the young men for their time and went on his way. "I have a feeling that I'll be seeing more of you two. Good day to you both!" Hector was confused by the man in black's prediction, but he was more concerned with the money Jamaal owed him. *"That Gringo must be lost. Now give me my money, son!"*

The man in black continued on his way until he reached his new home. St. Michael's Roman Catholic Church was located on Innis Street, which stood directly opposite and parallel to the overcrowded public Port Richmond High School. St. Michael's, founded in 1887 by four Jesuit brothers, was the only Catholic Church in a three mile radius. It once flourished as one of the most beloved and successful parishes on Staten Island. However, over the past fifteen years, the parish became outdated, the number of parish families decreased and it was in jeopardy of closing. That's why the man in black, Father James Malloy, was sent. Father Malloy was known in the New York City diocese as a "church healer." He did not heal lepers or raise the dead; he raised money. In his last position, he helped one parish raise over three million dollars, which enabled the church to keep its doors open for the following two years. But Malloy was not only a successful fund raiser; he was also someone who wanted more. He truly believed that he could transform parishioners into doing marvelous things. Surveying the neighborhood with light brown eyes, Malloy finally located his new home.

Upon reaching the steps of St. Michael's, Father Malloy noticed that the gothic-style church needed some attention. Overgrown weeds jutted out of broken concrete and dark green moss attached itself to faded brick. Despite the lack of upkeep, the priest did notice the beauty of the parish. The church possessed magnificent stained glass windows, which allowed a great amount of light to penetrate through the building. James Malloy always felt that the stained glass windows were the most beautiful parts of all Catholic architecture. The reflective and decorative glass windows depicted religious scenes and stories of the Bible. One frame caught his eye. It was a depiction of the famous artwork, *The Good Shepherd,* which is one of the earliest findings of Christian art. It depicts Jesus carrying a lost sheep among His flock. The priest took in a deep breath and considered the art work. Malloy then wondered how his new flock would receive him. This thought engrossed Malloy as he didn't notice the sound of heels clapping against the tiled floor.

As Malloy entered the hallowed halls, he was greeted by an elderly woman, standing only five foot tall. "Good morning, Father. My name is Alice Pritchard and I am the church secretary." While she had a pleasant demeanor, her eyes told another story. She was analyzing and critiquing this new pastor and did not seem overly impressed. "Are you aware, Father

Malloy that you are the third senior priest they've sent in only two years' time?"

"How do you do, Alice? I am aware of that fact. I would agree that being the third pastor in three years does sound alarming. Is there a reason why the other priests did not stay for the long haul?"

Alice was surprised that this priest was interested in her opinion. The last priest that presided over the church seemed to know it all. He had all the answers and would never ask the church secretary her opinion over the state of the parish. While this was a step in the right direction, Alice was not convinced. Narrowing her eye lids, she replied, "Some people don't want to get their hands dirty." Father Malloy understood what she meant and nodded to her in agreement.

"Father, you best get ready because your first celebration of mass will be at noon, today."

"Thank you, Alice." The priest dipped his head when he said his goodbye. He exited the parish doors.

Father Malloy had a few hours before 12:00, so he decided to go and investigate the new neighborhood. One of Malloy's vices was coffee. He so loved drinking coffee that he often claimed that he would gladly accept an IV drip of Folgers or Maxwell House. He always put a little more sugar than one should, and he even drank it at night. Occasionally, the priest would have trouble sleeping on account of the coffee, but the risk of sleep deprivation did not deter the cleric from his beverage of choice. With a cup of Joe on his mind, Malloy decided to venture out into his "new" neighborhood.

This new position for Father Malloy was an exciting one, but the place was not exactly new to him. The cleric spent his high school years in a neighboring town. Port Richmond had not changed much, but if it did, it seemed to be on the decline. "It's more depressed than I remember," Malloy thought to himself as he casually meandered up and down Port Richmond Avenue. He saw dilapidated buildings, old hardware stores, and bodegas on several street corners. The people had rugged faces adorned with dark bags under their eyes. Their hands seemed swollen, almost sausage like, from hard labor. Most of the men wore stained jeans, long thermal undershirts, and firm work boots. Malloy could tell he was in a blue-collar town with people who probably faced adversity daily.

"Hey *muchacho,* who are you?" A deep and gruff voice shot from across the store. It was the owner of the small store, Eduardo Nunez, who spoke broken English. Father Malloy walked towards the man to greet him, and extended his hand. "My name's Malloy, I'm the new priest at St. Michaels." The store owner looked at his hand as if it were lost and replied, "I wonder how long this one's going to stay?" Nunez shook his head and laughed smugly.

Father Malloy was quickly realizing that he was going to have to earn the respect of the people. At his last position in Brooklyn, the people would bow down to the priest without him uttering a single word. He was revered before he even gave his first homily. Malloy always felt awkward when people treated him as if he was some holy man who had special healing powers. He was just a man trying to do a job as best he could. "Just like anyone else" he would often say to himself.

Father Malloy was curious if the store owner knew about the church's sports program. Malloy was hoping there was a

6

baseball, soccer or basketball team. "Excuse me, Senor Nunez, but do you know if St. Michael's has any sports teams?" "Ha! They've got a team alright – basketball. But if you watch them, you would never know it. They haven't won a game in two years." Malloy was taken aback. *Two years?* That was an awfully long time to go without a victory. This fact certainly piqued the cleric's interest, for basketball was one of the priest's passions.

Sports invigorated the priest. He was a natural athlete. Standing only 5'9", he was average by most standards, but he had a great motor. He ran for his high school track team and set the Staten Island record in the 100 meter dash. He always credited his speed to his father, who was known to run away from trouble. Once, his father told him that he outran the thugs and the police in the same night. Malloy's talents were also physical gifts. Malloy had peculiarly wide toes. He always likened himself to a fleet-footed hare. Malloy always used his powerful feet to accelerate and burst passed competition, much like a rabbit does when pursued by falcons and foxes. Malloy thrived in any running sports. Naturally, football, baseball and track were strong suits. Of all the sports he played, however, his greatest love was basketball. He loved the idea of a team working together in unison to achieve one common goal. He always felt that basketball was a sport where you had to be in sync with the other players on the court. To Malloy, sports like baseball, while entertaining, were too much in isolation. There's a pitcher and a catcher and a whole lot of waiting. Malloy disliked the idea of individual achievements. What mattered most was whether or not the team won. That's not to say Malloy didn't earn his own individual awards. When Malloy played for Port Richmond High School, he set a high school record of assists and he averaged 14.5 per game. Malloy loved being able to split a defense and help a teammate score the ball. Helping others score was a goal. However, Malloy's personal glory came when he stole the ball from ball handlers. Being able to shut down a rival point guard by beating the man to a spot on the floor gave Malloy great reward. There was no greater rush than the thrill of swiping the ball from the offensive player or from blocking a difficult shot. Another physical strength of Malloy was his strong legs. Malloy was able to touch the rim ever since he was 15 years old. He used his 'hops' to block players who towered over him. His coaches often praised his defensive leadership and used Malloy as an example of how defense can turn into offense. Malloy had learned the game from a pastor in his neighborhood. Rev. Gerry Mosley, a Baptist preacher, took the Irish-Catholic under his wing and nurtured him in basketball and in life. Mosley taught Malloy the value of discipline and hard work. Despite the fact that Malloy was not Baptist, or a member of the congregation, Mosley gave up his free time to help the future priest. Malloy promised himself that he would undertake the same life mission when he was given a congregation of his own.

Malloy knew one way to make a dent in the neighborhood was to get the basketball program off the ground. Basketball was the favorite sport among teenagers in the Port Richmond area. He knew there was talent in this neck of the woods. Unfortunately for Fr. Malloy, there was no school at St. Michael's. It was merely a struggling parish. Fr. Malloy knew he had to get to work fast. And speaking of fast, Malloy had to get back to the church for his first celebration of mass.

Chapter 2 –

"As you think, so you shall become."

– **Bruce Lee**

Meanwhile…

Hector Ruiz was sitting in his 12th grade English class. Hector detested English more than any other class. In his mind, having to read books and write essays was pointless. To make matters worse, Hector was being forced to read *Hamlet*, which meant reading William Shakespeare. "This language is for idiots, man!" Hector announced to the class. These outbursts came often and with great fervor. "Congratulations Mr. Ruiz, you just earned yourself a detention slip." These words were commonplace for Ruiz as he was not very interested in school. To make matters worse, the bespectacled teacher announced more great news: "Next month, we will be reading another Shakespeare tragedy, *Romeo and Juliet.*" - More grinding and gnashing of teeth!

Hector had failed his English class last year and he had to attend summer school to make up the credit. Even in summer school, Hector was resistant to learn. It wasn't that he couldn't learn, but he just was not interested in school. All he wanted to do was play basketball. He was a great point guard and he wanted to be just that eight days a week. When he tried out for the Port Richmond varsity team, he astounded the coaching staff and was placed on the team, despite being a freshman. It was very rare that a freshman would be placed on varsity. Junior varsity was the designated team for underclassmen.

However, after three games into the season, Hector's report card was delivered and he was no longer allowed to be on the team. Failing subjects eliminated high school students from participating on sports teams. Due to this fact, Hector took his game to the streets where he tried to hustle older, more advanced players. Despite his age, he was able to work on his business skills and amass over 300 dollars per week hustling other "ballers."

After school, Hector played again for money. This time, he took on a white kid from Port Richmond. His name was Mickey Sullivan – an Irish-American boy in the same grade. Mickey was not fast, like Hector, but he could shoot with his eyes closed. He was blessed with long branch-like arms and when he set for a shot; his arms perfected a graceful follow-through which usually resulted in a "swish." Sullivan's sweet spot was around the three-point arc. He would practice these types of shots daily and it certainly was the strength of his game. Even though he was a lights-out shooter, the rest of Mickey's game needed work. His defense and lateral movement was awkward and undisciplined. Hector was well aware of Mickey's weaknesses. As they began their pick-up game, Hector dashed and darted to the hole where he was able to hit short range jumpers and high percentage lay-ups. Mickey just didn't have the athleticism to keep up with the Mexican boy. Mickey hit his share of shots, but in the end, Hector won the match and 35 bucks.

As nighttime fell upon the court, Hector remained there, alone. Hector was like a worker on an assembly line. He would shoot the ball, retrieve the ball, and shoot again. It was obvious that the young man was infatuated with the sport of basketball. This was an escape from the difficulties in his life, and he became very good at it. After hitting five jump shots in a row, a vibration went off in his pocket; it was his cell phone. *"Hola, my love!"* It

11

was Hector's mother. "Come home, *ahora*!...I made you your favorite dinner - *arroz con chuleta*." Hector's appetite was certainly growing as he expended a great amount of energy defeating Sullivan. "Ok *Mami*, I'll be home in ten minutes."

As he was walking home, he saw the man in black walking towards him. Hector rolled his eyes and tried his best to not make eye contact as they passed. It didn't work. The man in black approached the teenager with a warm and inquisitive voice. "Excuse me, son, but are you the boy who I watched playing basketball earlier today?" "I'm not your son." Father Malloy wasn't expecting a rude response like that, for he hadn't crossed the boy at all. "I apologize if I offended you, but I wanted to complement you on your ball handling." "What do you know about basketball, *Gringo*?" Malloy knew that being called a '*Gringo*' was not exactly a compliment. He could tell the boy was not in a mood to play. "Well, I might know more than you think. Your defensive work, for instance, is sloppy."

"My defense is what? Did you really say that, old man? I'll mop the floors with you and all your nuns." Hector chuckled to himself, even though he knew keenly aware that he was outright disrespectful.

Trying to diffuse the tension, Malloy jokingly retorted, "Hey, the nuns I know would likely foul out for hitting." A brief smirk appeared on the Mexican boy's face and he continued on his way. Malloy didn't want to push the first encounter any more, but as the two departed, a knowing smile appeared on the good friar's face. Malloy was setting the foundation for a future encounter.

Undeterred by his encounter with the priest, Hector continued walking home. He was feverishly striding home desperate to give his mother the money so as to help out. Reaching the house, he skipped every other step and bounced on into the house. "Mami, this is for you." Hector pulled a twenty-dollar bill out of his pocket and handed it to his mother, Esmeralda. Esmeralda, an attractive woman of forty three years of age, looked at her son with loving eyes. "*Gracias, mi amor!* Now, do I have to ask where you got it from?"

"I worked an extra shift with Jamaal…honest." "Ok, as long as you're not getting money in a bad way! Now, let's eat." Hector loved when his mom cooked. She made pork smothered with Adobo seasoning with white rice and avocado. It was one of his favorite meals. Hector's mother was always running low on cash, on account of her husband, Pedro, passing away three months prior. Hector's father had been working in the New York City subway system and he suffered a heart attack late one night. It was a devastating blow emotionally and financially. Hector's father had made decent money, but his life insurance and presently, the life insurance money was running out. This created a great strain on Hector's mother, who was always trying to make ends meet. Whenever Hector thought about his father or his mother's financial state, he became angry.

This all meant that Hector was now the man of the house. It was his job to take care of his mother. He was an only child and his mother, Esmeralda, was his entire family. Esmeralda owned a small dry cleaning store on Port Richmond Avenue that barely paid the ever growing bills. She was holding on to the store as best she could. However, the rent was beginning to overwhelm any profits the store was earning. Life was a burden and the tunnel produced no light.

St. Michael's

Father James Malloy was excited. He knew what he wanted to do and was determined to get his great idea off the ground. He asked to meet with the current Catholic Youth Organization (C.Y.O.) coach of St. Michaels. The man's name was Raymond Garvey. Last season, under his direction, Garvey won a grand total of zero games. It wasn't that Raymond wasn't a great coach; it was that he was a terrible coach. It wasn't his entire fault, though. As a matter of fact, he was actually doing the parish a favor. It wasn't easy to find volunteer coaches these days, especially when men and women work six and seven days a week. Father James Malloy's predecessor was grateful that he had Garvey just so he himself did not have to attend the games.

"It's a pleasure to meet you," Father Malloy announced to Garvey. "Same here, father. You wanted to meet with me?" questioned the squat and bald-headed middle-aged coach. "Yes, I did. I have a great interest in helping out the basketball squad and I was wondering if you would consider adding me to your staff." Garvey had to take a step back. Garvey couldn't' believe that the presiding pastor of the parish was asking to work under him. As impressed as Garvey was, he actually had other plans. "Father Malloy, I am deeply honored that you would be willing to work with me on the team, but the thing is, I really hate basketball. I only did this to help my nephew, George Garvey, last year. If someone didn't coach the team, it would have dissolved. I really only did it for him. I'm sorry but, I really do not want to be a part of the team anymore. The team is yours, Father."

"I completely understand. I would like to thank you for your dedication to your nephew and to the basketball team. I hope I will see you this Sunday at mass. "Uh….yea sure Father." The man left in great relief.

Once Malloy was alone, he made a firm fist and pumped it with great vigor into the air. "Ha!" Malloy was invigorated and overwhelmed with joy knowing he would coach the team. The next move for Malloy was to set up C.Y.O. tryouts for the 12th grade team. Little did any of the parishioners know, Malloy had big plans for this high school team.

Chapter 3 –

"Give me six hours to chop down a tree and I'll spend the first four sharpening the ax."

– Abraham Lincoln

Sunday mass – 10:30 a.m.

The parishioners at St. Michael's entered the pews as custom. Most were looking at the new priest with the eyes of pessimism. Who was this new priest anyway? Would he leave so quickly like the others? Would his sermons be interesting? Would he have any personality at all?

Father Malloy knew the people would be looking for a leader-someone to follow, but he also knew they wanted sometime to care about. His first homily focused on prayer and belief in God.

Father Malloy's began his homily:

There's an old story about a man who believed God would save him from a flood. He stood at the top of his house and waited for God to save him. First, the Navy came with a life raft asking him to jump in, but the man refused them. "No, God will save me!" The waters rose higher and then the Coast Guard arrived. They sent a rope down a helicopter. Once again, the man did not leave his home. "I have faith; God will save me!" Finally, the Air Force came to save him on a plane. The man denied the help once again saying, "God will save me!" Well, as you can imagine, the waters overwhelmed the home and the man drowned. Upon entering heaven, the man humbly spoke to God, "Lord, I'm so grateful to be here in paradise, but I have a question. Why didn't you save me?"

God looked at the man for a brief moment and said, "My son, I sent you the Navy, the Coast Guard and the Air Force." My brothers and sisters, God will be there for you, but you need to look for him in all places."

A hearty laughter echoed the church walls as Father Malloy's homily was a hit. The cheerful response invigorated the priest as he felt trust and faith growing in his flock. Fr. Malloy was grateful to gain a feeling of acceptance from the parishioners in the parish. The success of the sermon almost made Malloy forget about his final announcement, but Jamaal Jordan's face in the back pew jarred his memory.

"We have one final announcement: There will be tryouts for the 12th grade C.Y.O. basketball team this Tuesday."

After finishing the masses for the day, Father Malloy decided that it would be a good idea to knock some of the rust off of his game. Off went the black and white outfit and on went sweats and Converse blacktops. He walked to the gymnasium with pain in his knee and back. "I'm not seventeen anymore," he thought to himself. Once, he had been the quickest, fittest, and finest defender in the city. But that was a long time ago. He still possessed a trim and athletic figure, but he certainly lost a step. It was not an easy thing for Malloy to accept the fact that he wasn't as athletic as he once was. Now forty years old, he had more grey hairs than he'd like to admit. As he was taking jump shots and worked on his ball handling skills, he concocted a plan for the tryouts.

St. Michael's Parish – Tryouts C.Y.O. – Senior Division

Flicking on the lights of the gymnasium at 8:30 in the morning, Father Malloy was optimistic for the outcome of the day. With just a little luck, he would form a team that would compete against other teams in the C.Y.O. division. This was not his ultimate goal, but it would be a starting point. Unfortunately for the vicar coach, the turnout was underwhelming. Nine teenagers showed up. This was disappointing to Malloy, but at least he could spend the two hours evaluating what he had.

"Hello Fr. Malloy, my name's Joey Tucker. I can't wait to play basketball. I've never been on a team before." Malloy could see the excitement in his eyes. If his game was half as big as his heart, he would have a player on his hands. Father Malloy shook Joseph Tucker's hand and gave him a pat on the shoulder for encouragement. Then, he began to address the others.

"Good morning, boys. If you don't know me, my name's Father James Malloy. It's an honor to be with you all today. I know we didn't have a great season last year, but if you all are willing to give your best, I promise we will have better results this year."

"Hey Priest, where's the coach?" – A voice called out and echoed in the parish gymnasium.

Father James Malloy looked each boy in the eye and announced, "You're looking at him."

The boys looked at the priest as if he had just performed an exorcism.

"Whaaaaaaaaaaaat! This is whack!" – Henry Patterson was not amused. Henry was a giant of a teenager. He looked both puzzled and angry at the announcement. This was the overwhelming thought in the room.

18

"Excuse me, but you're a priest, not a coach." The voice came from a muscular boy walking in late. It was Jamaal Jordan. His sarcasm was easily detected. "We will be a laughing stock if we got a priest as a coach. What are we gonna do, pray during layup drills? Or maybe we'll have baptisms at half-time."

The Sanchez brothers thought this was good time to pile on. Pablo declared, "Yea, if we miss a shot, do we have to go to say three Our Fathers." His younger brother added, "How about, if we win we can skip church on Sunday."

Malloy nodded at the boys' frenzied humor and decided to chime in on the situation. "Hmmm…How about, if we win a game, we take a picture, because that hasn't happened in two years."

"Ooooooooohhhhhh," the boys hollered using a mocking tone.

Malloy could see on the boys' faces that they had doubts on his level of expertise. "Believe it or not, I used to be a player way back in the days of the dinosaurs. Now, I've done some research and it seems as though this team hasn't won a game in some time. Sometimes in life change can be a good thing."

"Now before we begin our practice, I would like for us to all learn a new prayer." If looks could kill, these teenage boys would be putting this coach six feet under. *Here we go,* Jamaal thought to himself.

Now, we all attend St. Michael's church. So I think it's appropriate if we learn and say the prayer to St. Michael:

Saint Michael the Archangel,
defend us in battle.
Be our protection against the wickedness and
snares of the devil.

Amen.

"That sounds awfully serious," one boy announced. Then Joey Tucker jumped in bewildered, "*Snares of the devil...What does that mean?*"

"Boys, it is important to know where you come from and where you are going. We are St. Michael's parish. It is imperative for all of us to know about our namesake saint. St Michael is an archangel, which means he is in the highest rank of angels – like a general in the army. And just like a general, he was chosen to drive out the forces of evil from heaven. He is known for his honor and strength in battle. Take a look at the image of him atop the façade."

A painting rested atop the façade leading to the outer doors. It was a painting of Michael-the archangel, sword in hand, standing over a snake. The artist portrayed Michael as a powerful force of good striking down the enemies of heaven. Father Malloy was hoping each player could bring their own strengths to the team.

"If you play with the discipline of an angelic soldier, we will win many games." The spiritual words silenced the critics for a time. Father Malloy figured it was a good time to begin teaching his basketball philosophy.

"Ok, enough theology for now. Let's play some ball. Now, everyone I want you to line up in one line at the baseline. The first test is defense. You cannot win any game if you don't play defense. So this is what I want to see."

Father Malloy then spread his arms wide and began sliding his feet. He zigzagged across the court, shimmying from baseline to the half court line and then shuffling from half court to the other baseline. "Watch me; look at what I'm not doing. If you notice, I'm not crossing my feet. If you cross your feet, you will not beat the offensive player to the spot. You could also stumble and get tripped up. Now, let's go."

Watching the first drill was tough for Malloy. The boys were not very athletic, all except Jamaal Jordan. He was not exactly fast, but he was an athletic player, able to move well for someone of his size. He couldn't keep up with the likes of Hector, but he would certainly overmatch other boys his size.

Another pleasant surprise was the shooting of Mickey Sullivan. While not fleet of foot, he impressed Coach with his three point shot. All over the court he was setting up for shots and knocking them down. He reminded the priest of a modern day Steve Kerr – a three-point specialist who played with Hall of Famers Michael Jordan, Scottie Pippen and David Robinson.

The weakest player seemed to be Joey Tucker. Unfortunately, his game did not match his enthusiasm. When Malloy moved to ball handling drills and foul shooting, it got even worse for Tucker. The ball seemed to weigh 100 pounds in his hands.

Tucker, though, was the least of Malloy's problems. None of the boys seemed to have the ball handling skills to run the point-guard position – Malloy's position. He would work on their skills to improve, but by 17 years old, many habits were set. He needed to find a point guard.

The following day, Father Malloy posted the Senior Division Team. Malloy kept notes on the practice:

Notes:

Peter Thomas – *Decent speed; poor shot; seems to be a backup point guard*

Jamaal Jordan - *Quick feet; good rebounder; strong post-move ; needs a pat on back*

Joseph Tucker – *Heart of a winner; very little basketball skills – need a plan for him*

Mickey Sullivan – *Tremendous shooter; outstanding range; slow a foot; poor defense*

John Montgomery - *Possible center; can block a few shots; not much else*

Mario Sanchez – *Possible shooting guard/small forward – long stride, long arms*

Pablo Sanchez – *Mario's brother; same skill set; but left handed*

Christopher Medina – *great defender; reminds me of me; not much offense*

Henry Patterson – *hit every foul shot; slow-a-foot; offensive replacement at end of game*

After practice, Father Malloy called Jamaal over to him. "Jamaal, I wanted to talk to you about your buddy I saw you with the other day. We could really use a ball handler on this team. What's the story with him?"

"Oh, Hector..he ain't gonna play for this team. He used to play for Port Richmond until he got thrown off the team. Failed off , 'na mean?"

"I understand."

"Why should I help you? Ain't that your job?" It was obvious to Father Malloy that Jamaal wanted to be on the team, but he wasn't going to show it. He was going to keep pushing and pushing until Malloy proved himself.

"Listen, Jamaal, I have big plans for this team. We have some good parts to this team, but we need that point guard leading the offense. Trust me, we would all benefit if Hector joins us. Can you ask him to meet me here after school tomorrow?"

"Aight…I'll tell him."

Chapter 4 –

"Be more concerned with your character than your reputation, because your character is what you really are, while your reputation is merely what others think you are."

– John Wooden

Hector did not look all too interested in what Jamaal had to say. He did, however, mention that he would be the starting point guard. This would be an opportunity to play the whole game, fill up his stat sheet, and maybe he could make a tape for scouts. He saw dollar signs in his eyes as Jamaal explained that there really wasn't any competition for him at the point.

As Hector was waiting for the eighth period bell to ring in World History class, he felt another vibration go off in his pocket. *"Llama me pronto*, Hector." It was his mother. Raising his hand, Hector asked the history teacher if he could go to the bathroom. In the hallway, Hector found a small corridor and called his mother. "Hector, I lost the laundromat." Hector clenched his teeth and closed his eyes with a furrowed brow. Now, his world was going to get even more difficult. "What do you mean you lost it? What did you do?" Esmeralda became even more upset as her son was berating her with accusations. Hector began struggling with the problems in his life. *"Why can't my mother just pay the bills? Why do we have to be damn poor? Why did my Papi have to die? I hate everyone!"*

Leaving the school, he noticed Father Malloy standing outside of the church. Begrudgingly, the young boy walked over to the priest hoping for a quick two minutes meeting. Hector was hoping for a "Hey, great to have you, see you tomorrow," and then he could be on his way. However, Father Malloy had other plans. "Hector, is it? Come on in, I'd like to talk to you about the team."

"Well, I really gotta go. I'm on the team right?"

"Yes, if you want to be, but please let me just take five minutes of your time."

Huffing and puffing a bit, Hector entered the church.

Father Malloy wanted Hector to feel wanted, but he also wanted him to know that he had to tow-the-line if he wanted to remain on the team. "We would love to have you. You're an exceptional point guard. However, in this life, talent is not enough. You must be on time. You must be respectful to your teammates and to me. Do you agree to these conditions?"

"Yea, sure, whatever you say." The priest's voice was coming across as white noise. Suddenly, Hector was intrigued by something other than basketball. He noticed the priest had just cleaned several gold chalices and a six-foot silver cross. Hector had dollar signs in his eyes.

"Hey, Father, are you always here at church ….umm…Sometimes, I feel like I need someone to talk to about my problems, you know?"

"Well, I'm certainly here to help you. I'm here for the most part, but some parts of the day I'm out tending to the flock."

Malloy was hopeful that he could get through to the angry young man. "I'll tell you what…If I'm here at church; I'll hang rosary beads outside the doors. If I'm not here, I'll take them with me. That way you'll know."

"That's really great of you, Father!" An impish grin appeared on Hector's face and suddenly he had to get going. "Oh, Father, I've got to run. My mom needs me."

"Ok....Practice starts tomorrow at 3:30 pm."

Knowing his mother was probably in great distress over the loss of her job, Hector scurried home. Upon entering the house, Hector found his mother with mascara running down her face. It was obvious she was crying as she had make-up filled tissues in hand. "Mom, what happened?" Hector was concerned, but his voice was stern and rigid.

Looking down at the ground and palms up in the air, Esmeralda confessed to Hector. "I haven't been able to pay the rent. The landlord shut us down. I need to pay $600.00 to pay off the debt. And even if I could pay the debt, it will just continue. I don't know what to do. We need more money!"

Hector wanted to feel compassion for his mother. He wanted to embrace her and show the love he had for her. He wanted to be a good son. But his anger and frustration overwhelmed him. The love he wanted to show were in the dark shadows of emotional pain. He began shouting expletives and his empathetic eyes turned wicked. "Must I do everything in this house! I'm only 17 years old. Why can't you take care of your own crap! I'm sick of this!" This only exasperated the fractured tone of the house. Already emotional, Hector's mother lost it. She couldn't listen to one more hateful word. "Get out of here right now! Get out of here, Hector. You ungrateful *burro!*"

Hector stormed out of the house full of steam. His eyes like those of a wild man. He thrashed around the streets of Staten Island haphazardly. Hector's needed space and he wanted to think. While he walked passed Ralph's Ices, a popular attraction for teenagers and families on the island, he couldn't help but notice other families with fathers, brother, sisters and fancy cars. Why did he have to have such a difficult start to his life? Why couldn't he be born into a better home, a better family? Hector's anguish continued and there was nothing he could do about it.

The only consolation for Hector was that the weather was cooperating. It was a mild 60 degrees in the cooling month of October. Hector knew the basketball team at Port Richmond would still be practicing. He figured he could sneak in and sleep there for the night.

He walked back to his school, but the doors were locked. There was no way in. Hector forgot that it was Monday, and that all the teachers had meetings. As a result, there were no practices held on Mondays. Angry now at himself by his oversight, he set his sights on a new building – the church. Hector was not really into attending church, but he heard that the doors were always open. That wasn't always the case in this day and age. Many parishes on the island began locking their doors after many thefts occurred. Luckily for Hector, Father Malloy believed people should be able to worship God 24 hours a day, seven days a week. However, the rosary beads that Malloy spoke of were missing, which meant Malloy was busy 'tending to the flock.'

Hector decided to spend the night at St. Michael's. His plan was to stash himself in the dark, "quiet room" in the back of the church designed to sit the crying babies and rambunctious youth of the parish. The small parish held a draft and was quite chilly. "Cheap priest", Hector figured. Though uncomfortable, Hector grabbed a religious book resting on the mahogany book case. He rested his head on top of the thick texts. Then, he laid down on the short area rug. He took off his black bubble jacket and used it as a blanket. It was ironic that in a place meant for saving, Hector had now felt as lost as ever.

Chapter 5:

*"Winning is not a sometime thing, it's an all the time thing.
You don't do things right once in a while…you do them right
all the time."*

– Vince Lombardi

The church bells rang loudly at 7:00 am. Father Malloy was
preparing for 7:30 mass. The dark room holding the boy
remained so. Hector noticed someone on the altar; it was
Malloy. The lost teenager hid himself as best he could behind the
door of the crying room. Hector was nervously eying Malloy,
hoping he would leave. Father Malloy was preparing for mass.
The priest opened the good book to the first reading. Silently
mouthing the words of the reading, Malloy rehearsed his work.
Malloy's homily was based on Jesus' parable of the tax
collector. The tax collector was a great sinner, but he asked for
forgiveness and because he was contrite, he was forgiven. The
priest hoped that, like the tax collector, his point guard would
find humility. Hector had no clue that he was on the priest's
mind.

Watching from afar, Hector's moment finally came when the
padre went to the back vestibule to put on his ceremonial robes.
Hector moved with great stealth; he made no sound and
methodically began his exit. Something, though, stopped Hector.
Something caught his eye. It was a pristine golden chalice. The
chalice would fetch Hector a king's ransom. There was no
hesitation. Like a thief in the night, Hector swiped the cup and
exited the solid oak door of the church undetected.

The first thought that came to Hector's mind was to go to Terry Spinner, who was one of the leaders of the gangs in school. He was a member of the *Snipers,* who always dressed in camouflage. Terry rarely attended school and was far more interested in the playground where the majority of his transactions occurred. Hector was confident that a guy like Terry would be interested in the chalice. Nodding his head to the side, he motioned for Terry, a giant of a young man – standing almost 7' foot tall, nonchalantly strolled over to Hector. Hector and Terry knew each other since they were in elementary school. While their friendship was no longer a strong one, they were both cognizant that they both came from the same place. That meant that they always showed each other respect.

In a quiet voice, Hector described his new merchandise. "Hey man, this is pure gold. It's a treasure I'm sure you and your buddies would like to have." The Mexican boy was bluffing a bit, not sure if it truly was all gold.

Examining the chalice with a close eye, Terry seemed to be impressed. "I've seen a lot of these in my day. I can tell you this; the cup is 32 carat gold. On the black market, it's probably worth 800 dollars. I'll give you five bills for it."

"I need at least six."

"Make it $575.00 and that's my final offer," replied the more experienced businessman.

"Fine...It's a deal!"

Cautiously, Hector placed the golden cup back into his black backpack and zipped it shut. He then handed the backpack to Terry. There was a place in Hector's heart that felt extremely guilty for stealing and then selling a religious item. But, there was only one thing that ruled Hector's world: money.

Once the backpack was resting on Terry's shoulders, the two teenagers embraced in a disguised hug. While protected by each other's backs, Terry slipped Hector the money he had been promised. It might as well have been thirty pieces of silver.

"I'll be seein' you, boy," Terry smiled as he left for the school yard.

"Yea, sure whatever man." Hector wasn't really listening to Terry. He had dollar signs in his eyes and wretchedness in his heart.

Practice:

Father James Malloy was pacing up and down the court at St. Michael's. He was anxious to get practice started. Today he wanted the team to focus primarily on defensive strategy. This was his strong suit and he felt that it was a skill he could pass down to the team.

One by one, each member of the team started entering the gymnasium. Father Malloy set up water bottles for the boys to drink after the practice. Some of the boys noticed and thanked the priest.

"Everyone I hope you are doing well today. Let's start with a silent prayer." The friar led the team in silent prayer and then ordered the team to begin stretching their leg muscles in preparation for an intense workout. Malloy knew it was not prudent to run without working the muscles. Many great athletes over the years recommend working up a sweat before a big match and Malloy couldn't agree more. Unfortunately, the team was one player short, Hector Ruiz.

The time was 3:47 when Hector arrived. He nonchalantly strolled in and acted as if nothing was the matter. The team was in two lines working on layup drills. Hector jumped in line, but was immediately disciplined. "What do you think you're doing? Get off the line right now!" Suddenly practice stopped as the team began watching the coach vs. the pupil. "What's the problem, priest?" Hector's cavalier attitude didn't sit well with the padre.

"You're late; that's the problem. If you would like to participate today, I'm going to need you to apologize to your teammates and run ten laps around the gym. In addition to the laps you will stay an extra 17 minutes to make up for your tardiness."

Hector sucked his teeth, dropped his head, and sported a wicked smirk on his face. "You have to look tough in front of the team," Hector announced and then he laughed to himself. "Make it twenty laps." Begrudgingly, Hector leisurely trotted around the court. Then, Malloy began to speak to the team; he did not wait for Hector.

"Gentlemen, during last week's tryouts, every one of you gave a strong effort. Each of you has an area of strength and an area of weakness. The teams that play the best are the ones who utilize the strengths of their players. It is also important that we work hard every day turning our weaknesses into strengths. We will eventually come across an opponent who will be able to take away our strength. We need to sharpen our weaknesses so that we can rely on them in times of need. I want to tell you a story that will help you understand what I mean."

The Priest continued, *"Once there was young buck living in the woods that had the most majestic antlers in his entire herd. The other bucks were in awe of his beautiful antlers, but they often teased the deer because he had very thick legs. While muscular,*

33

they were not the gracefully narrow legs other deer possessed. Well, one dark evening, a pack of hungry wolves entered the buck's dominion. Startled by the predators, the buck became stuck in the thicket. His mighty and majestic antlers were tangled up in the tough branches. It did not matter how hard he twisted or pulled. He was unable to escape. Then, with the wolves approaching, he relied upon his ugly, but powerful legs. He dug his powerful legs into the cold tundra. With great force, he was able to break free of the thicket and the wolves. The deer's most recognized talent was a weakness, whereas his least admirable feature ended up saving his life. Can you see what how this can help you on the court?"

Pablo Sanchez, one of the clowns of the group responded comically. "So, you want us to play like Bambi?"

"Very funny, Pablo, but what was the point of the story?" Malloy wasn't sure if his message penetrated.

Joseph Tucker came to the coach's aid, "You want us to be good all-around players, right?" Malloy gave a knowing smile, seeing something special in Joseph and concurred. "Yes, Joseph. This can also help you in life. If you work hard on your weaknesses, whether it is a certain subject in school, or a relationship in your life, if you work at it, it will become an area of strength." The boys began nodding their heads understanding that this little lesson was about basketball and about life. Maybe this coach was more than meets-the-eye.

Father Malloy felt that he could challenge this group.

"Now let's talk about trusting each other when we play defense. One of the most effective defenses is called the "zone defense." Playing a zone means that each player is responsible for

defending an area of the court, instead of guarding one individual player.

When we are playing a zone defense, you must trust that your teammate will cover his assignment. If you over-commit and leave your assigned zone, the defense will not work because you will be opening up a gaping hole for the offense to exploit. For example, if Mickey does not trust that Jamaal will be able to defend his position down low and leaves his area to help, he is actually leaving the outside perimeter unprotected. Conversely, if Jamaal does not trust that Mickey can cover his area, and leaves the basket area to defend a player, we will the rebound. In order to play this defense well, we all need to trust each other. Now, let's practice this!"

The players were working together and trying their best to resist leaving their zone. This is the hardest part of playing zone – demonstrating patience, honoring your zone, and having chemistry with your teammates. When an offensive player is dribbling out of your zone, you must have to the self-discipline to trust your fellow teammate to take over defensive responsibilities.

The players were running in and out of defensive line ups. Christopher Medina seemed to have the potential to be a dominant defender. He was super quick. Medina would often beat the offensive player to the spot he wanted to go to. Malloy was excited to have a defensive stopper. Medina reminded Malloy of himself when he used to play. Malloy was even given a nickname based on his defense – "Robin Hood" – because of his thievery on the court and because of his philanthropic nature off the court.

This brief stroll down memory lane was quickly erased by Hector Ruiz. To Malloy, Hector was frustrating to watch. On the one hand, Hector would demonstrate supreme ball-handling, blazing speed and cat-like reflexes. On the other hand, the point guard would dribble the ball endlessly around in and out of the zone. Hector figured he was the best ball handler on the team and as a result, he should be the one with the ball in his hands. His talent was obvious, but so was his problem. Father Malloy stopped the play and asked to speak to Hector privately, while Peter Thomas led the offensive team.

"Hector, I need to talk to you about something."

Hector swallowed hard. *He must have seen me in the back of the church. I'm ready to punch this guy and bounce.*

"Hector, what do you think your teammates think of you when you practice like you have?

With some confusion, Hector responded: "What do you mean?"

"Listen, Hector, you are a very talented ball handler. However, when you dribble the ball for that length of time, you lose momentum and your teammates are not involved. There are times in a game when we all need to lean on each other. If you don't work for your teammates, why should they work for you?"

"Who cares? I hit my shots didn't I? Hector made his point and thought he would shut up the priest for good.

"That is true; you did hit your shots today. But things don't always work out so perfectly in the heat of a game. You need to know that every player on the court is willing to make sacrifices for the good of the team. That means that sometimes you will have to pass the ball to an open player. You're going to have to have faith in others besides yourself."

36

Hector was matter-of-fact when he answered the priest back. "Yo, man, I'm the best player on this team and you know it!"

The players looked at each other with disappointment in their eyes. The Sanchez brothers sucked their teeth. Jamaal looked down and shook his head.

The priest quickly realized that leading this flock was going to be harder than he thought.

Father Malloy ended practice and told everyone to be back the next day to learn the offensive system.

As everyone was changing to leave, Father Malloy asked Hector to stay for a few minutes. Hector, once again, rolled his eyes but agreed.

The priest knew that the boy wanted fortune and fame, so he decided to go about the talk from a different angle. An old basketball story came to his mind that would help chip away at Hector's selfish play.

"Hector, who is the greatest basketball player of all-time?" The priest asked already knowing the answer.

"What do you think- I'm stupid – Michael Jordan, of course."

"Yes. And did you know that even the greatest of all-time had to earn the respect of his team. One way Michael Jordan did that was the night he came back to play the New York Knicks after he had retired. "

"Oh yea, the "Double-Nickel" game; he scored 55 that night."

"Good memory! But what you may not remember is the ending of the game. The great Michael Jordan, who scored 55 points and dominated the floor, trusted his teammates to win the game for him. In the final moments of the game, he was double teamed by two Knicks defenders – John Starks and Patrick Ewing. Jordan passed the ball to their offensively challenged center, Bill Wennington, who was open for the score. Jordan could have taken the more difficult shot, but he realized that the chances of victory were far greater if he trusted his teammate. Wennington hit the game winning shot. It all came down to trust. Do you understand?"

"Yea, yea, yea….Pass the ball." Hector's tone was less aggravated.

"No," the priest replied firmly, "Trust the team." Malloy could only hope his words were chipping away at the stone.

How odd it was for the priest that the person whom he was teaching about trust had just robbed him blind.

Chapter 6:

"If what you did yesterday seems big, you haven't done anything today. "

– Lou Holtz

After practice, Hector and Jamaal were walking home. The two were chatting about girls, annoying teachers, and just about how everything was going in their lives. As they strolled down Morningstar Road, Jamaal was curious about Hector's take on the new coach.

Jamaal began questioning Hector about the new coach: "Yo, man, what do you think about having a priest as a coach?"

"It's weird. I mean, he's not that bad. Sometimes he thinks he has me all figured out. What do you think about that dude?" Hector was opening up to Jamaal and asking him how he truly felt. Jamaal was one of the few people he trusted enough to be honest and open with. They had known each other since kindergarten, but it had only been recently that they rekindled their friendship.

"I actually like Father Malloy a ton. He seems like he really wants us to do well. I don't think he means any harm. Oh, you know what I forgot to tell you, he helped me out the other day. I was shooting hoops after school, like usual, and then Ms. Reynolds came over busting my chops about my critical lens essay. That's the one with the quote in it. Well, Malloy saw that I was looking all frustrated. I told him about the essay and he showed me how to do it. He even introduced himself to the teacher and I think he scored me some brownie points. I'm gonna get my grade on the paper tomorrow. We'll see if he knows what he's talking about."

"Oh, that's pretty cool." A heavy feeling struck Hector's stomach as he thought about the golden chalice that he stole and sold. His mother needed the money. *That's why I did it,* he would repeat to himself. However, trying to rationalize the immoral decision didn't help. He had stolen from someone who had shown him generosity and trust. To make matters worse, he had stolen from the church. His mother would be devastated if she found out the truth.

Considering his terrible decision, Hector was thinking about consequences. "Do you think there really is a hell for the bad people?" This was a strange topic for Hector to speak on, but Jamaal shared his thoughts on the matter.

"Uh...yea I guess. They talk about it in the Bible." – Jamaal looked at Hector with eye-brows raised as he was surprised at the new talking point. "All I know is that I don't want to end up there, you know."

In a low tone, Hector replied, "Yea...same here." Hector didn't know where he'd end up, but he did know that he was one step closer to being locked out of the gates of heaven.

"Alright man, I gotta bounce; this is my stop!" Jamaal clasped hands with Hector and embraced each other by patting each other's back.

The walk home was a good twenty minutes. It gave the thief plenty of time to think about his transaction. He frequently looked left, right, and over his shoulder while he fingered the dollar bills in his pocket. It was a sin to steal, for sure, but at least he was helping his family.

"Yo, Mami! Where are you?"

"En el bano...Un momento, por favor."

As Esmeralda exited the bathroom and walked into the kitchen, she could tell Hector had something on the tip of his tongue. "What is it?" she asked inquisitively.

"Here, this is so you can reopen the business." Hector pulled out six one-hundred dollar bills and handed them to his mother. He was sure the Laundromat would reopen tomorrow.

"*Dios mio!* Where did you get this money?" Esmeralda was more alarmed than overjoyed.

"I sold my baseball cards to a collector. My Roberto Clemente rookie card got us over $400.00. Now, you can reopen the store."

"Oh my God, this is amazing my son. But, I cannot use this money for the business. This is your money. Besides, even if I did find $600.00, I have to pay for the rent and for groceries and gas for the car. I would need to use it for the bare necessities before I tried to reopen the business."

Though Esmeralda was speaking logically, all Hector heard was the sound of ungratefulness. Growing angry in a flash, Hector raised his voice. "How much money do I have to bring you? I solved the problem right now and you won't use it for the business?"

Shaking her head and pushing the money towards her son, Esmeralda had a bad feeling about this money. It was almost cursed. She knew she couldn't keep it and she had reservations about where the money actually came from. She refused to take

42

it, but then Hector took the money in his arms and threw it at Esmeralda. The hundred dollar bills lay orphaned on the floor.

Despite his great anger, Hector knew it was up to him to make money. He was going to have to back to the well.

Sunday

Standing at the pulpit for his third week as pastor of the parish, James Malloy began to gain confidence in his impact with the church. Father Malloy liked to hold rosary beads his grandmother had given him before her passing. He held them out of habit and they always put him at ease. However, Malloy was feeling much more at home at St. Michael's as the days passed. He had already set up a program to help women who had been left by their husbands or boyfriends. Malloy was also able to secure state funding to feed the children of those women. St. Michael's though, had many generous contributors. The food donated to the battered women was homemade –*fresh chicken, baked potatoes, green beans, and stuffing.* They also made the most delicious desserts. For instance, Mickey Sullivan's mother, Jean, made the most divine Irish-soda bread you would ever eat.

Sunday mass

For today's homily, Father Malloy wanted to speak to his flock about the importance of prayer. He wanted to use this famous Irish joke to set the tone for his sermon.

There once was an Irishman named Flanagan. He had a very important job interview at 9.00am in the morning. Flanagan had been running late and needed to find a parking spot outside. The chances of finding a spot in time were bleak. That's when he decided to pray to God. He said, "Lord, if you can find me a

43

spot right quick, I promise I'll be good and attend mass every Sunday for the rest of the year." Well, no sooner than those words passed his lips, he found a parking spot from the heavens. Then, he finished the prayer by saying, "Oh... Lord.....Never mind! I've found a spot!"

Brothers and sisters, it is important to speak to God. It is also important to realize that God is sometimes in the details."

Joseph Tucker listened attentively to Fr. Malloy's homily. He wanted to impress Father Malloy, so he decided to wear a white button down dress shirt with a straight black tie. Tucker continued his spiffy look with newly polished shoes. He looked like a million bucks, except when he sat down, you could see that he was wearing white socks instead of the formal black. Father Malloy saw this from the altar and chuckled to himself. The priest was impressed with Joseph's efforts. Tucker waited for everyone to greet the priest after mass so he could speak to him one –on-one.

"Father Malloy, that homily you gave was wonderful – just dynamite!"

"Oh, Joseph, thank you so much. I hope you will be on the lookout for God's graces, unlike my Irish friend, Flanagan. How's your left-handed dribbling coming along?"

"Not very good, Father. I know I'm not really good, Father. I want you to know that you don't have to feel badly if you don't play me that often. I know I'm the worst on the team. It would be best if others played instead of me."

Tucker's words stopped Malloy in his tracks. He knew what the boy said was true, but he didn't expect a teenager so young to be so critical of himself and so selfless in requesting less playing time. Malloy wished he could take Hector's talent and somehow inject it into Tucker's body. Tucker had the attitude of a winner – someone who thought of others before himself. Malloy felt that Tucker was underutilized. Malloy lifted his hand to his chin and began to rub the stubble on his chin. "You know, Joseph, I think there's a position I'd like you to consider."

"What's that, Father?" Joseph straightened himself and was now on his toes with his eyes wide open – he smelled an opportunity might be coming his way.

"I really haven't any assistant coaches. I have zero team managers. There's no way I can do this job all by myself. How would you like to be the team manager and assistant coach?"

"Are you serious? Of course, I'll do it! Thank you, thank you! I won't let you down." Tucker was as light as a feather. He felt as if he was finally a true member of the team.

"Now, this isn't going to be an easy position. You will have to organize our travel plans, contact parents, and possibly even scout the opposing team. Are you sure you're up for this type of work?"

"I promise you; I can do it." Joseph was sure he would be successful in this position.

"And if I hear anything about your grades dropping, I'm putting a kibosh on the whole experiment. Is that clear?" Father Malloy's tone was firm; he wanted Joseph to know that this was a serious offer.

"Yes, sir, um...I mean father...err...I mean, Coach." Tucker could barely get any words out. He managed to thank the priest nervously.

"Ok, go and tell your parents the good news." A wry smile emerged on Father James Malloy's face. He was grateful to have such a pure-hearted pupil in Joseph. Malloy had no idea that this decision would pay major dividends down the road.

After many gracious words from the parishioners, Father Malloy was left alone in the empty church. It was times like these when he became lonely. Being a priest meant that the people shook your hand, thanked you, and revered your homily, even if you didn't deserve the praise. But when the dust settles, the priest would be alone. There were a few traveling priests who would come and celebrate some of the other masses, but Malloy was the primary clergyman.

James Malloy began thinking of Monsignor Peter Petrillo, who served as his mentor at St. Joseph's seminary in upstate New York. Petrillo warned Malloy that loneliness is a part of the profession. Sometimes he wished he had a family of his own. He wondered what profession he might seek out if he ever decided to leave the priesthood and have a family. He knew that he loved sports and loved working with young people. Naturally, a teacher came to mind. He also considered psychology. Analyzing the mind and the human behavior was intriguing. In any event, Malloy was left to his thoughts.

To combat his idleness, he decided to diagram some offensive plays for his team. Malloy wanted the boys to focus on defense first, as it often leads to offense if executed properly. Malloy's offensive philosophy was built on movement and precision. He believed in back-door cuts to the basket, setting hard picks for teammates and by out hustling your opposition. "It is the only way to beat superior talent," Malloy often said to himself. One aspect that he did not like about basketball was the isolation systems that were being put into place around the country. So often, he would watch college and professional players take their best player, give him the ball and move out of the way. It was basically a *mano-a-mano* battle. To Malloy, however, there was no strategy involved. *Was that really strategy? Was that a great game?* Malloy never enjoyed watching the eight other players on the court gawking at two players going one-on-one. Malloy thoroughly enjoyed outwitting the opposing coach by using his keen eye extra motor. He turned the tables on those coaches who lazily disregarded the entire five players on the court.

In the first play, called "Host", the point guard would bring the ball up to the top of the key. Then, the shooting guard would run as fast as he could around two picks. One pick would be set under the hoop by the power forward and the second would be set by the center on the opposite side of the paint. The shooter would escape unscathed and be open for a mid-range jumper. One of the keys to the play was making sure that both low post players didn't remain in the paint for three seconds, as that would result in a three-second violation.

At times Malloy was consumed by the sport of basketball. However, Malloy was well-rounded, well-read, and had many interests. One such interest was fishing. Malloy decided to make the most of his leisure time, so he decided to head down to the Staten Island pier. The priest dressed himself warmly, packed a few beers, and grabbed his fishing pole. The cleric did not have a boat to go on, so he would have to fish off of the wooden pier. Malloy was sure to take his transistor radio, as he loved to listen to sports talk radio or classic rock and roll. Good tunes and good fishing was a heavenly combination for the good friar.

Father Malloy packed his gear into the beat up silver Chevy Cavalier which was donated to the parish years ago. The last three head priests had also used the sturdy, yet worn vehicle. The priest made a stop and the local bait shop, *Terry's Tackle Box,* off of Hylan Boulevard, and drove to the dock by the bay. It was brisk out and there was a terrific wind blowing. There wouldn't be a crowd today, maybe a month ago, but not in the increasingly unpleasant weather. The gray clouds and chilly weather usually kept the "Sunday fisherman" away. When he arrived, there were only two other men working their rods. Father Malloy casually walked up to the pier with his rod, his bait, and his beverages. He took out a sharp hook and attached a live worm. Malloy then cast the hook into the murky waters. Fishing was a peaceful way for Fr. Malloy to clear his mind when he needed to, or search for wisdom from the almighty. Often, the good priest contemplated life, the delivery of his sermons, and now his coaching techniques. He wondered if his own father was looking down upon him with pride or disappointment. Malloy was seemingly much different from his own father. Edward Malloy was always interested in acquiring money- always trying to get a quick score. Malloy thought his father would be proud that he turned out to be a morally sound individual, but part of him wondered if his father would think him too simple and too content with an ordinary life. Sometimes ordinary people can do extraordinary things. Malloy hoped the basketball team would be one of those examples.

Chapter 7 –

"You can't win unless you learn how to lose."

– Kareem Abdul-Jabbar

Some boys were tying their shoelaces while others stretched. Jamaal was cradling the ball with both hands deep in thought. St. Michael's senior C.Y.O. team prepared for their first match of the season. Father Malloy called for his team to go into a huddle. The team walked over to the priest with their hands on their hips. "Ok, now, just like we practiced. Work hard on defense. Trust each other and stay in your zone. When we get turnovers, sprint down the court and look for high percentage shots. That means attacking the rim. When we are on offense, work the angles and set firm picks. Let's win this first game!"

The schedule makers didn't do any favors for Father Malloy as St. Michael's had to being their season against the C.Y.O. runner-ups from last year's junior division- St. Patrick's. The opponent's court was full of cheering parents, which sent echoes throughout the gymnasium. This road game was going to be a good test for Father Malloy's progress. One obvious obstacle St. Michael's faced was the opposition's home court advantage. The brilliant green of St. Patrick's was seemingly everywhere and the parents had wide eyes expecting a win. Then there was St. Michael's. Their black and gold team was supported by a few single parents in the visiting area. It was evident that St. Patrick's had a culture of winning and St. Michael's did not.

St. Patrick's traditional white and green jerseys resembled the Boston Celtics. These colors were pristine and the jersey numbers and last names of the players were stitched into the jersey. Malloy admired the colors of his family's Irish heritage. Since St. Patrick's was home, they wore their Kelly green home jerseys with white trim.

St. Michael's colors contrasted with St. Patrick's, as they donned white away jerseys with black numbers and gold trim. These jerseys were screen printed on – much less professional than St. Patrick's professional looking garb.

Game 1: St. Michael's vs. St. Patrick's

Coach Fr. Malloy sent out his starting five. He decided to start Hector Ruiz at the point. Fr. Malloy wasn't sure if he earned that spot, yet he was the only one who could break down a double team and a full court press. At shooting guard, he started Mickey Sullivan. Sullivan had great range and was the best pure shooter on the team. At the small forward position, Malloy had another tough call. He could go with either Sanchez brother, who were athletic and had some offensive game or he could go with Chris Medina, the shut down defender. Father decided to go with Medina because he had caused several turnovers at the last practice, including one against Hector. The power forward position was held by Jamaal. Jamaal's size, rebounding skills and low post moves made him a formidable player. Finally, Malloy started John Montgomery at center. The priest figured giving Jamaal another rebounder down low would help out the team greatly.

At the tipoff, St. Michael's got off to a hot start. Hector crossed over his defender on the first three trips down court and scored each time. They were out to an early 6 – 0 start. The defense was holding tightly in zone. The starting five were sliding their feet, honoring the zone and their responsibilities. The players on the bench for St. Michael's couldn't believe what they were seeing. They had to rack their brains for the last time they were leading any game, let alone a game against the second place team from a year ago. But some things are short lived. Antonio DeShields, St. Patrick's best player – their small forward – went off. He blew by Mickey Sullivan for an easy layup on one possession. Then, on the very next one, He hit a three point shot off of a screen. It was obvious that he was the reason for their success. These back to back plays knocked St. Michael's back to reality. As fast as you could say *Jack Frost,* Father Malloy's game plan fell apart. St. Patrick's began hitting shots and St. Michael's began to abandon the game plan. To make matters worse, the star point guard became extremely selfish. Indeed, Hector had taken and hit the first three shots, but then he had also misfired on the following five shots. It seemed as though Hector was more concerned about his own stat line than the one that mattered the most- *the win column.*

Father Malloy had to call a time-out. He subbed Hector out for Peter Thomas. Peter jumped in and tried his best, but he was struggling against the press. Despite this fact, Malloy kept him in the game. As the game entered the second period, Malloy questioned Ruiz: "Hector, we can't have you taking every shot. You need to get others involved. If you take the shot every time down, we are predictable and we are not sharing the ball. I need you to help your teammates score."

Malloy was perplexed when he heard Hector's response, "Dude, you suck. You can't play. I'm the one with the skills." This was disappointing and unacceptable behavior. As the coach, Fr. Malloy benched Hector for the remainder of the game. This was also embarrassing for the priest and for the boy as mothers and fathers watched the pupil disrespect the teacher.

St. Michael's lost its first match of the season, 58 – 47.

This was not how Fr. Malloy envisioned his first game as coach. "I guess if it were easy, anyone could do it," Malloy thought to himself. He tried to focus on the positives. Mickey Sullivan went 7 – 9 shooting and ended with 19 points. Also, Christopher Medina had three steals. The Sanchez brothers combined for 14 points and 14 rebounds. They were good all around contributors. However, it wasn't good enough, because they didn't play well enough together.

Monday morning:

The alarm clock rang and Hector hit the snooze button again and again. Esmeralda entered his room and shook him. She pestered him until he finally made his way to the shower. Hector had little to get excited about. His life was unraveling at home, on the court and in the classroom.

Hector's English period was once again, painful. "Mr. Ruiz, can I see you for a moment?" – Hector's English teacher firmly requested at the end of first period. The bespectacled man with a receding hairline was holding a paper in his hand. It had red marks all over it.

After the bell rang, Hector reluctantly remained in his seat as his classmates moved on to the next class. "Hector, I have something for you. This is your test on *Hamlet*. You did not do so well. As a matter of fact, you failed with a 58%. This is your third straight failing grade. If you don't pick it up, you will not graduate. You will be left back."

"Teach, I told you, I HATE Shakespeare." Hector was being honest and forthcoming. "This stuff is boring as all hell and the language is stupid."

"Whether it is or not is not important. What is important is that you start passing some tests, otherwise I'll have no choice but to fail you for the year."

Hector's demeanor was beginning to change. His stomach was like a fireplace and every word the teacher spoke was like kindling – the flame was starting to take shape.

"Yo, you better pass me. I'm not staying back here next year. This place flat out sucks. I hate this school, this class, this subject, this idiotic story; EVERYTHING!" Hector yelled and cursed and thrashed his graffiti-filled marble notebook in front of the frustrated teacher. "I'm outta here!" Hector stormed out of the classroom. The class became silent as they were shocked and awed at Hector's angry fit. Hector abandoned his English class and then exited the high school. He had cut out for the rest of the day.

It was a blustery October day, with forceful cold winds. Hector stuck his hands in his pockets to try to stay warm. He was hoping to go back to the church so he could get a hold of that silver cross, but Father Malloy had the rosary beads dangling in the wind.

Hector needed another plan. He began to walk to the corner bodega on Innis Street. Entering the store, you could see his breath in the cold wind. Despite the cold, Hector bought a 'Yoo-hoo' chocolate milk. He had always loved the taste of chocolate milk. Even though he was older now, he still found a small piece of joy in the bottle. Those nostalgic thoughts soon were replaced by feelings of greed. A tenth grader named Juan

Castillo walked into the store. Juan was a diminutive boy, standing only 5 foot 3. He was thin, but he appeared larger because of his sweatshirt and cut-off bubble jacket. Hector stalked his prey and watched carefully and quietly. When the younger boy looked around the store, Hector would look down pretending to read the backs of canned food. Finally, Juan picked up a pack of gum and requested a pack of cigarettes. The grizzled cashier did not even card the teenager. It was obvious that there was no way Juan was 18 years old. Nevertheless, Juan pulled out a wad of cash. It was wrapped in a rubber band. The folded cash looked, in Hector's estimation, to be over two inches thick. Hector quickly exited the store and waited for the younger boy to emerge.

When the boy finally exited the store, he opened up the pack of cigarettes and dug into his pocket for a match. Hector nonchalantly walked up to the boy and then pretended to stumble into him. While the two bodies were entangled, Hector secretly removed the cash from Juan's pocket.

"My bad, son," Hector held up his hand to the boy in apologetic form. The boy gathered himself, but did not retaliate. Hector had seemingly escaped the encounter undetected. "It's like taking candy from a baby," Hector thought as he hurried home.

Sometimes in life, it is important to research your opponent. Hector knew the boy was quiet, small and an easy prey. But what he didn't know about Juan was that he was the newest member of the Snipers.

Hector was impatient. The money was burning a hole in his pocket. Being quite quick, Hector leaped up the staircase, jumping over two steps each time, to his secluded room. He was finally relieved to be alone. $328.00 was the amount. This time, though, Hector was going to keep some money for himself.

He still had to pay for his C.Y.O. basketball jersey and plus he decided that he wanted to walk the streets comfortably.

Leaving some money on the kitchen table was Hector's way of apologizing to his mother for his constant outbursts. He caught a glimpse of himself in the mirror. His face seemed to have two sides. On one side, he looked like the man he wanted to be, providing for his house. But the other side was shamed, stealing from the church, from someone who cared about him and now, from a younger boy.

Chapter 8:

"The best way to find out if you can trust someone is to trust them."

– Ernest Hemingway

The fall season was turning bitterly cold with frost freezing over car windshields. The teenagers at Port Richmond high school were sporting their red sweatshirts and sweatpants exiting school. The team made its way over to the gothic church. The rosary beads were hanging for the boys to see. Fr. Malloy was getting ready for practice by running suicides alone. As the boys entered the gymnasium they were impressed at the vigor and speed at which Malloy was running. He ran as if he was participating in a race against a ghost running next to him.

He was sweating profusely. His St. Michael's gold colored sweat shirt had a ring of sweat at the top of the collar. Finally, with the entire team, including Hector, watching, he asked them to take a seat.

It took a great deal of humility and patience for Father Malloy to not go off on his star point guard. He decided that Hector was used to the typical "screaming-at" reaction. It was time for another approach.

"Boys, you played very hard for each other and played well during the early part of the game. One reason why we were unable to win was because you began to ignore your assignments. You know it's very easy to work hard when you're winning, but it's very hard to stay disciplined when you're losing."

The priest continued, "We do not always have control over the scoreboard, but we do have control over how we act towards each other. And, I am not convinced you all care for one another. Therefore, I have devised a test. I need two volunteers."

The first person to volunteer was of course, Joseph Tucker. He was always eager to help out of please the priest. The other person to come forward was Henry Patterson. It was quite a contrast having the diminutive Tucker standing next to the mammoth Patterson. Father Malloy then unfolded two chairs and placed them in the middle of the court.

"Please sit." Malloy then took out two handkerchiefs and told the two players to cover their eyes with and tie a knot around their head. They boys folded the cloth so that only their eyes were obstructed.

Father Malloy then went to the kitchen and brought out an apple and an onion. The rest of the team was fascinated as they huddled around the coach and the players. "Boys, in my hands I hold an apple and an onion. Here, smell each so that you know I am telling you the truth." Each boy took a turn smelling the apple, a golden delicious, and a Spanish onion.

"Ok, we are going to see how much you care about the person next to you. Now Joseph, I want you to take both apple and onion, smell which one is which, and I want you to keep the one you would like to eat and give Henry the one you want him to eat."

Grumbling and excitement emerged from the rest of the team. Every eye was as wide as dinner plates. Joseph Tucker smelt the food in each hand. Meanwhile, Henry was nervous, fingers pressed against his knees. Tucker made his decision and placed the food into Henry's hand.

The priest's next demand was as follows: "Now Henry, take a bite."

"Crunch!" It was the delicious and sharp sound of an apple on teeth.

"Thank you, Lord! And thank you, Tucker!" Henry was pumped to have been given the apple. He hugged Joseph Tucker and a bond was formed.

"Ok, now Joseph, you know what you have to do."

Tucker knew that he had to own up to his end of the bargain. He began to lift his hand close to his mouth when a loud voice bellowed across the gymnasium.

"STOP!" Father Malloy yelled at the top of his lungs. His goal had been reached. Hopefully, the rest of the team would begin to believe in each other. Malloy considered moving on to a scrimmage, but he wondered if he could push the test a bit further.

"Before we let Tucker eat the entire onion, will anyone here help Joseph finish it?"

After a few moments of silence, Henry stood up and told the priest that he would split it with him. Then, Mickey stood up and walked over to Joseph and agreed to take a bite. And one-by-one, the teammates agreed to share the load – even Hector. So Fr. Malloy went back to the kitchen, retrieved a cutting knife and split the onion up. He handed each player a piece of the onion and he himself took the largest remaining piece for himself. With eyes tearing and grimaces on faces, each player chewed and downed the rough herb.

"This is friggin' gross bro!" declared John Montgomery. And the defensive wiz, Chris Medina, couldn't stop the tears from welling up in his eyes. The teammates began ragging on Chris and any other player who began to cry. "Ha! Go cry to your granny!" The well-devised test was a success, and Malloy looked on with an approving grin. Father Malloy couldn't help but think of when Jesus celebrated the Last Supper with his disciples. Malloy, like Christ, was unifying his team albeit in an unorthodox way.

After running defensive drills, Malloy put an end to the practice. He told the boys to arrive at the gymnasium on Saturday at 12:30 sharp. The game was to start at 1:00pm against the defending champions, Our Lady of Pity parish.

As the boys were exiting the gym, Fr. Malloy asked Hector if he could speak with him in private. Hector was obviously uncomfortable as he folded his arms and seemed to be cleaning his teeth with his tongue.

"Hector, I want you to know that I want you on this team. However, we have rules. One of those rules is to respect me as your coach and as a priest. The way you spoke to me was unacceptable and it was embarrassing as the entire crowd saw the altercation. I'm going to need you to agree to follow my directions and to listen to my input as your coach."

Hector was hoping this talk would end as soon as possible. He was nodding his head up and down and his body was leaning towards the door. The priest tried to get through to Hector, but he could tell the boy was merely trying to get on with his day. "Sure, I'll be a better listener," he told the priest disingenuously.

Game #2: Our Lady of Pity vs. St. Michael's

Freezing rain poured down on the black tarred parking lot outside of St. Michael's church. Players and family members hurried inside wearing yellow rain coats and straight brimmed baseball caps. The people were stomping their feet and swiping their wet sneakers on the large welcoming matt. Father Malloy greeted his players and the opposing players as they entered. He couldn't help but notice the disparity of team colors. This was St. Michael's home opener, but you would never know it. The black and gold jerseys of the home team were certainly in the minority. The visiting team, Our Lady of Pity, dominated the gymnasium with baby blue jerseys. Father Malloy and his players were strangers in their own land. If St. Michael's was to ever have a true home-court advantage, they were going to need more fans. This thought was on his mind, but Malloy had to put them aside for the time being. He had a game to coach.

Malloy deployed the same starters as from the first game. However, he substituted Mario Sanchez for John Montgomery. Mario had two solid weeks of practice and was more athletic than Montgomery. This would mean that Mario would play the power forward position. He was undersized for that position, standing only at 6' 1, but he made up for that lack of size with long arms and a strong motor. Malloy knew Mario would lose a few rebounds, but he also knew he would accumulate steals and blocked shots. Besides, Malloy figured he would save Montgomery for later on in the game in case Jamaal found himself in early foul trouble.

Our Lady of Pity was certainly a formidable opponent. They won the C.Y.O. Junior Division the year prior and currently sported a 12 – 1 regular season record. Their best player was Lance Thompson, who was a slashing small forward with a great long range jump shot. He was almost impossible to guard one-on-one and he always wound up on the line shooting two – if you were lucky. Father Malloy had scouted him in his last game against St. Claire's, as he scored 27 points and pulled down nine rebounds. Malloy had also been studying the team's box scores in the Staten Island Advance – the borough's newspaper. It seemed as though the shooting percentages of the point guard and shooting guards were below 40% in their last three games. So Father Malloy devised a plan to stack the box with his defenders. He wanted them dropping back a bit in the zone, giving some room. He was basically daring the defending champions to take three point shots.

At the outset, it was a very physical game. The referees were allowing tough inside contact. This was to St. Michael's advantage, as Jamaal and Christopher were able to strip the ball and block shots without getting into foul trouble. On offense, the smaller and quicker unit was running up and down the court with great ferocity – it was as if they were running from the bulls in Spain.

Hector, who did not yet apologize to Father Malloy, was scoring, but at a cost. He was taking the majority of the shots, and was passing the ball sparingly. Father Malloy was debating whether or not to bench Hector. Hector didn't truly deserve to be out there, but he was Father Malloy's only true point guard. Malloy went against his gut, and kept him in the game. The priest was influenced by the eyes of his players.

It was uplifting for Malloy to see the players' faces on the bench. Their eyes were slowly growing wider and wider; they were beginning to believe that they could knock off the defending champions. But the Our Lady of Pity team did not become champions by accident. Lance Thompson, their star player, was having a field day against St. Michael's. He started the game five of five from the floor. Fr. Malloy knew that Thompson was going to get his share of points, but he also knew that pretty soon, he would start to miss, just like his teammates. As they entered half-time, the score was tied at 42 all.

"We are following the game plan perfectly!" exclaimed the invigorated head coach. As long as you hang in there and stick together, there isn't anyone on this island we can't beat!"

Every player had a gleam in his eye, except one.

As they opened the third quarter, Our Lady of Pity brought the full-court press. Instantly, things began to change. The pressure placed by the other team caused poor ball handlers like Mickey Sullivan to turn the ball over. As a result, Hector was dribbling the ball way too frequently and constantly attempted "coast-to-coast" scores. When a player does indeed go from one end of the floor to the other, he expends a great deal of energy and in turn, does not involve other teammates. It seemed to be the same old story for Hector. This put Fr. Malloy in a tough position. He was his one true point guard on the team, and he was a selfish one at that.

The priest called a time out and subbed in the Sanchez brothers and Peter Thomas. While very much undersized, this unit would at least be able to break the press with their strong ball handling skills. The team, despite facing adversity, was hanging tough. They were down only four points entering the final period.

"C'mon guys, we can do this!" announced a serious and focused Joseph Tucker.

As the fourth quarter began, they started to hit their stride. Mario Sanchez ran around two great picks set by Jamaal and

Henry and hit a great 12 footer at the top of the key. Then, Jamaal hit a shot on a fade away – reminiscent of New York Knicks great, Patrick Ewing. Then, Mickey Sullivan drained a key three-point shot to come within one point of the lead. With ten seconds left, and the ball, St. Michael's was down by one.

Father Malloy called a time out. He concocted a play that would bring Jamaal to the top of the key. Jamaal would set a pick for Hector. If Hector's defender and Jamaal's defender went with Hector, he was to dish the ball back to Jamaal, who would be open for a jump shot. If Hector was free, he would drive the lane, try to score or dish to a crashing Pablo Sanchez from the baseline.

Mickey Sullivan inbounded the ball to Hector. Hector crouched down low and began to dribble. 9....8...

Jamaal came up, as instructed, and set the pick for Hector, 7....6...., Hector drove past Jamaal...5....4...

The defenders stayed with Hector 3.....Hector did not pass the ball to Jamaal...2....He pulled up and shot over two defenders....1......the ball swerved around the rim two full rotations and then rimmed out. Final score: Our Lady of Pity 67 – St. Michael's 66.

Chapter 9:

"Even if you fall on your face, you're still moving forward."

– Victor Kiam

The loss was a tough pill to swallow, especially because they followed a perfectly constructed game plan until the very end. It took but one selfish play by one individual to spoil the efforts of the entire team. Several of the players were growing tired of Hector's decision making. While the priest was settling payment for the referees, one player, Peter Thomas, let him know how he felt, "Way to blow it, dude. You had Jamaal wide open."

"Yo, shut up scrub. Go back to the end of the bench where you belong," Hector responded forcefully. Hector was shocked that Peter verbally attacked him. This set off a switch in Hector. There was a fire in his eye, one that he knew how to turn on.

"You're mad ghetto! All you care about is yourself. " Peter had a mouth on him and wasn't afraid to hold back.

Hector angrily marched over to Peter and stood face-to-face with him. It was if they were weighing in for a boxing match. "Do something, punk!" Hector demanded. "You're a corn!" Peter snickered at Hector's remarks. "And you're a ball hog… We would have won if you didn't screw up the last play!"

Jamaal decided it was best to step in and stop this feud before it became something serious. Using his large frame, he positioned himself in between both smaller players. This move proved to be quite prudent as the two began to reach for each other. The two rivals were unable to connect blows and the altercation came to an end once the priest entered the fray.

"Stop this at once! You're embarrassing yourselves, and this parish!" Malloy took Hector by the back of the shirt and pulled him off of Jamaal's back. Finally, both boys relented.

Hector did not want stick around for Malloy's judgment, so he left the gymnasium. But this time, he didn't leave alone. Three dark figures followed him outside the church gymnasium. Once Malloy finished reprimanding Peter for his mistake, he looked for Hector, but he was gone.

Hector began to walk home at a rapid pace. It was frigid out, so Hector stuck his hands deep into his bubble jacket. He felt butterflies in his stomach as he heard footsteps behind him. Hector was smart enough to know that he could be in trouble. He turned his head slightly and noticed three figures following him. Hector was racking his brain. *Why would they be following me?* After a long pause, his heart sank realizing that these three figures had something to do with the money he stole from Juan. He picked up his pace and began trotting at a pretty fast speed. This served as a signal to the three figures that they themselves did not go undetected. Consequently, the three young men transitioned into an all out- sprint to catch the thief. Like a pack of wolves, the three boys outlasted their prey. Hector was cornered. There was nothing he could do.

One of those figures was Terry Spinner. The other two were high profile gang members of the Snipers. Terry grabbed Hector by the front of his jacket and pinned him against a nearby wall.

"You robbed our brother, Juan. That was our money. Where is it?" demanded Terry.

"I didn't steal anything. What are you talking about?" Hector always tried to deny, deny, deny. But sometimes, you can't outwit another fox.

"You're lying! Guys, hold this piece of crap up." The other two teenagers held each of Hector's arms and Terry punched Hector right in his stomach. Air left Hector's lungs as he collapsed to the ground. Hector knew he was in grave danger now.

"This is for stealing from the Sniper tribe," Terry had a wicked look on his face. He ordered the other two boys to continue to hold him while he grabbed a metallic green garbage can that was sitting on the corner of the block. The sanitation garbage can weighed over 45 pounds and could potentially do serious harm. Terry lifted the can and was about to slam it on Hector's head when seemingly out of nowhere, a man in black appeared.

The man in black jumped in between Hector and the other gang members. As the garbage can was about to come down on Hector's face, Father Malloy ran to Hector and used his shoulder to redirect its fall. The can missed Hector's head by inches. Father Malloy sustained a stinging cut on his right shoulder blade. There was no time for Father Malloy to consider a minor wound. Imminent danger was upon one of his sheep and himself.

"Guys, get him!" Terry, the leader, demanded a beat down of the priest. Luckily for Father Malloy, his "priestly gear" served as a secret weapon. One of the Snipers cautiously spoke up, "We can't hit a priest. We'll go to hell if we do!" The other boy chimed in as well: "Yea, let's get out of here before he reports us to the cops." Shockingly, the gang members felt their conscience getting the best of them. They quickly dispersed and left Terry there by himself.

"You are cowards!" Terry screamed. But Terry was unfazed by the priest's garb. Terry was bigger and stronger than this man of the cloth. To Terry, Malloy was simply someone who got in his way- and anyone who got in Terry's way had to pay. At once,

Terry lunged at the priest, with first swinging wildly. Malloy was able to dodge and weave around the swings, but one did catch him in the eye. Malloy relied on the training his father gave him. His dad was always in trouble and seemed to need to know how to fight. Malloy, always a good student, would have made his father proud. The priest managed to block Terry's very next swing, and this time, Malloy caught the swinging arm and twisted it behind his back.

Fr. Malloy had some parting words for the tall gang member before he let him go. "Hey, you listen to me. Hector's a good kid. You leave him alone, or else. You understand!" The blood in Father Malloy's body was boiling. He had always been taught to be a pacifist, never to fight or harm others. *But God does want us to protect ourselves*, Malloy always reminded himself. Malloy let go of Terry's arm and pushed him away. The leader of the Snipers stumbled. "Turn the other cheek, brother," Father Malloy sarcastically exclaimed. Terry looked at the priest straight in the eyes. "We're not through, priest!" Embarrassed by the loss, Terry quickly vanished.

Hector was watching the entire scene in amazement. It took him a moment to catch his breath. He was stunned that the priest was able to hold off Terry, who was known to be one of the best fighters in the school.

"Are you hurt?" Fr. Malloy asked Hector as he helped him to his feet. "Yea, I'm fine. Where did you learn to fight like that?" Hector was impressed by the priest's reflexes and knowledge of fighting. "Well, my father was no saint. He had his share of tussles. So, one of the skills he passed down to me was how to stick and move, like a boxer."

"Why were those guys after you?" The priest wanted to know what type of trouble Hector was facing.

"No idea, man." Hector did not want to let on about the money or else the Malloy might be able to connect him to the missing chalice.

"Well, they certainly are mad at you about something. You look like the wind was knocked out of you. Let's get you home."

Hector pushed the priest away. "I don't need your help. Leave me alone."

The priest was shocked that he was turned away. Surely, Hector would be grateful for his help, but he wasn't. He just rebuked the man in black and scampered on home.

That weekend, the priest did not have to time to analyze the team's performance as he had several priestly duties. For example, at 4:00 p.m., he had to perform a marriage. Father Malloy had met with the couple for Pre-Cana and they seemed to truly love one another. He always enjoyed performing weddings. He was even invited by the couple to attend the reception, which he happily accepted. At the reception, Father Malloy began the festivities with a prayer and soon drinking, eating, and dancing ensued. Sometimes, these days were bittersweet. Malloy loved to see two people of the faith coming together before God. However, it did remind him of the great sacrifice he made. Once, Malloy dated a beautiful girl named Maria, who was very sweet. However, Malloy had a calling for the priesthood. It was one of the hardest decisions James had to make. His life, though, was meant to serve the Lord.

The next day…

At Sunday mass, the crowd was slightly larger than the previous week. It seemed that Malloy was indeed making a small dent in the community and the sheer influx of parishioners proved it.

Another reason for the larger number was because Father Malloy invited all of his players to attend the mass. He wanted his players to come to church and he felt that he could send a message to them from the pulpit. Jamaal, Mickey, the Sanchez brothers and the rest of the team sat in the front pew - everyone except for Hector.

It was nearing the Advent season. It was Father Malloy's favorite time of the year.

Sunday Mass

"One of the greatest parts of the Nativity story is the unique path of the three magi. The magi traveled long distances to visit the Baby Jesus. They also risked death by disobeying the Roman leader, King Herod. The magi were supposed to inform the king of the whereabouts of Jesus. They, of course, did not honor Herod's request. They put themselves on the line for something they believed in.

Imagine that! These men put everything on the line for someone they had yet to meet. This is one of the greatest acts of faith in the Bible. Sometimes, I ask myself if I would have the faith of the wise men.

Brothers and sisters, we need to think about believing in God and believing in each other. Let's think about our thoughts and actions as we move forward this week. Ask yourself: Have I ever put it on the line? Have I ever put faith into someone who needs help?

Faith is not seen. We cannot all be a doubting Thomas. We must, at some point, dive right in and choose to believe in something, even if it doesn't seem to make sense.

I am very blessed to have my own basketball team here today. I believe in them. I know for certain that if these boys put their faith into each other, the sky will be the limit. Let's think about those brave wise men this week. Let's keep our eyes fixed on that bright star, which will lead us to where we need to be."

The players were extremely proud to have been singled out at mass. Mickey Sullivan was beaming with a smile ear-to-ear. They felt pride, they felt joy and the bitter loss to Our Lady of Pity was seemingly behind them. For some reason they felt extra special as they were mentioned on the altar. They were spoken in the same words as the three wise men and of the Christ. Never in their lives had any of the players been given so much praise, especially after a loss.

Practice – Monday

Again, Hector arrived fifteen minutes late to practice. The team had already warmed up and was working on a new inbound play. Malloy was crafting a play that would help break the press with more ease and fluidity. "Ok, Hector, you know the drill. You have to apologize to your teammates, run 10 laps, and thirdly, remain after practice for the amount of time you were late."

"Sorry guys!" Hector yelled obnoxiously. He meandered around the court for his first lap.

The other players were growing tired of Hector's act. They all recognized that he was talented and that they would probably win more games with him than without him. But, at the same time, he was like a cancer. He brought morale down and sucked the life out of the team.

Again, Peter Thomas made his opinion known. "Yo man, just shut your mouth and do your laps. You cost us the game, man." This instantly infuriated Hector as he jetted from performing laps into Peter's face. Father Malloy blew his whistle and quickly interceded. He pushed Peter away from Hector and demanded that they both separate. Jamaal, yet again, helped save his friend from further damage.

"Alright, that's it! If you disturb this team's psyche just one more time, you're off the team. Is that clear?" Fr. Malloy, just like Peter, was growing weary of this act.

"Who cares? You aren't even a coach. You're a priest. You don't even know what basketball is, my dude. Go baptize someone; go to the river and baptize someone." Hector smiled and looked around for agreeing faces, but no one was laughing.

"So you really don't think I know anything about basketball?" questioned the man in black. The man in black was the man in gray today. He was dressed in St. Michael's sweats.

"Uh, duh? You're a scrub," laughed Hector. The team members wanted the priest to say something or do something. *Why was their coach always so patient? Would he ever step up to this punk?* Father Malloy could see what the other boys were thinking. It was painted on their faces. Malloy realized that it was time to put on a little show.

Father Malloy took the basketball and shoved it in Hector's stomach. "Ok hot shot! Here's the deal. You play me one-on-one. If you beat me, you can start every single game with no questions asked. And, to top it off, you can say if and when you want to be substituted out of the game."

"Ha! Alright, I like the sound of that!" declared the smiling Mexican.

"But if I happen to win, you have to keep quiet for every single practice AND you have to follow my orders without question. *What do you say Mr. All-Star?*"

"It's a deal. This is going to be like taking candy from a baby. Let's play to seven. Deal?"

"It's a deal. We'll play *winners out* scoring by ones." Malloy added. "Shoot for the ball."

Hector agreed and shot for the ball from the foul line. His shot was true and was given the ball first. On the very first possession, Hector showcased his ball handling skills as he crossed-over the priest and dashed to the hoop for an easy score. "That's one, pops. Winner's ball!"

Hector drove the lane for a second time, but this time, he pulled up for a jump shot. Malloy decided that it was time to unleash his well-documented defensive tenacity. The priest crouched low with his arms extended. Malloy's wing span was much longer than Hector's which limited the Mexican boy's range. Malloy moved well without the basketball. He shadowed Hector wherever he went. Malloy was equally as light on his feet and harassed Hector without fouling. Hector quickly realized this bet could backfire. Hector gave Malloy a head fake and then drove the lane. The priest, however, was up to the task as he used his "hops" to block Hector's layup attempt. The priest instantly gained control of the ball and laid the ball in the hoop to tie the score at one.

It's time to teach Hector a lesson he won't soon forget. Father Malloy was always taught to turn the other cheek. However, the priest was not going to let a learning opportunity pass by. Connecting religion and street talk, the priest gave Hector the business. "This is for the Father!" Malloy looked straight at the basket, went into the triple-threat position and shot the ball from the three-point line. The ball went through the hoop; nothing but net. The score was now 3 -1 favoring the priest (When playing by "ones" a three point shot counts as two points). Hector checked the ball back to Malloy and again, Malloy spoke up. "And this is for the Son." Malloy shot and hit from three-point range again. The lead was now increased to 5 -1. The other boys were smiling ear to ear. They were both fascinated and exhilarated at the secret talents of one Father Malloy. "And this is for the Holy Spirit," The priest, with perfect form, shot the ball from behind the arch and drained the final shot of the game. The entire team was cheering as they quickly realized that Malloy personified everything he has been preaching. Finally, a man who practiced what he preached.

Hector didn't like to be shown up, but he realized he had lost the bet. He wanted to be angry, but at the same time, he had lost to someone who ultimately wanted to help him. It was time to just shut up. You could even make out a quiet smile on his face, befuddled that the priest had so much game.

"You just got a whole lot cooler in my book," replied Jamaal Jordan. "Yea, Father Malloy, that was sick!" added a clapping Joseph Tucker. Then the man in gray was embraced by the entire team.

Chapter 10:

"A man who wants to lead his orchestra must turn his back on the crowd."

– Max Lucado

Hector acknowledged to the team that the priest beat him fair and square. Miraculously, he went on to apologize in his own way for playing selfishly. He really wanted the guys to like him and to trust him. "That was my bad. I wanted the glory, and Jamaal was open. I should have dished the ball out. That was a bad play." His teammates were impressed that Hector actually owned up to his transgression. Trying to imitate their patient and forgiving coach, the boy chose to sympathize and reassure their repentant point guard.

"Don't worry about it, man." Jamal sympathetically interjected. "If it weren't for you, we wouldn't have even been as close as we were. We're a team. We ride together and we die together."

"Wow, take it down a notch," Pablo jokingly added. The team all had a good laugh and seemingly pounds and pounds of anger, turmoil, and burden lifted off of Hector's shoulders. New and fresh thoughts entered Hector's mind, and he enjoyed them. *Maybe this team was more than meets the eye. Maybe the priest really did care about him. Maybe I can start getting my life in order.*

"Alright, bonding time is over. Let's get to work!" Fr. Malloy reminded the team why they were there. Father Malloy had many conditioning drills ready to go, but a good coach knows when to call an audible. He could see now that the team was coming together; maybe they were destined for greatness. It was time to bond in another way; it was time to bond on a higher level.

Malloy always tricks up his sleeve and he decided to break out a very important lesson that all the boys needed to remember.

"Ok boys…What I hold in my hands are rosary beads. They are very important to the Catholic tradition. Now, my grandmother, Amelia, prayed the rosary every single morning of her life. The rosary is about praying to the Blessed Mother. We will all pray "The Hail Mary" and then we will each line up and shoot 10 foul shots. Every time we do this, we will be honoring God, the Blessed Mother, and we will be trying to remember that when we are on this court, we represent St. Michael's church."

Puzzled faces emerged with this unique command, but deep down the boys knew that Malloy had a greater message. He wanted the boys to learn more about God, about each other, and about how to act on and off the court. Father Malloy felt that he was laying the groundwork for character and faith.

Despite the good priest's best efforts, Hector still had a problem. The Snipers had eyes on Hector and were looking for an opportunity to strike. Hector was nobody's fool so he would stealthy sneak out of class five minutes early to move to his next class. Or he would ask a few teachers if he could monitor for him so to avoid the populated lunch room. It was going to be very difficult to continue this way, but there was no talking Terry down. Once you crossed him, you were done for. He did steal that money and he needed a way to replace it.

Having this weight on his mind, the problems of English class were far from his thoughts. However, his teacher always made sure to bring the problem to the forefront of his mind. "Once again, Mr. Ruiz, you did not do any homework. As of right now, it is not looking good for the second marking period."

"Whatever," Hector would say aloud. But he knew his ticket out of Port Richmond High School was going to have to be punched by this English teacher.

Game 3: St. Michael's vs. Holy Child

It was the first of November, and there was a light layer of snow on the black pavement. The snow covered the windshields of the cars parked at Holy Child off of Victory Boulevard. This gymnasium was freshly waxed and it looked marvelous. It only reminded Father Malloy that he needed to get more funding to keep up with the Joneses.

Despite the superior facilities, Father Malloy felt confident about the game. His team had bonded and they were following his direction. The team was ready to move forward. It was still an oddity to people to have a priest on the sidelines, diagramming plays, and shouting out defensive assignments. At times, however, this oddity worked in St. Michael's favor. Holy Child's coach, Bob Stewart, was a devout Catholic and was sporting a shiny, gold crucifix around his neck. Father Malloy noticed that the opposing coach kept ducking his head and raising his hand to the priest – almost as if he feared him. This type of behavior was typical of years gone by. The priest, in years past, would basically get many perks for serving the people. For example, the priest would never have to pay for cold cuts or baked ziti at the Italian deli. Other times, the cleric would show his Roman collar to a police officer and he would escape the occasional speeding ticket. Those perks seemed to diminish as the years passed. But in some parts, the priest was still revered. Father Malloy had great respect for all of the opposing coaches, but Stewart was one of his favorites. Malloy felt that it was always more enjoyable to coach against a friend. Though both coaches valued each other as people, once the game began, it was all business on both sides. The game was quickly dominated by a mentally and physically energized point guard. Hector was moving around like his typical quick natured self, but this time, he was also distributing the ball to his teammates. The second trip down the floor was emblematic of things to come. He broke down his defender with the dribble and then drove into the paint. This time, instead of selfishly looking to score, he dished the ball out to the left wing where an open Mickey Sullivan hit an uncontested three point shot. This unselfish play continued for the duration of the game. Hector scored only nine points, but he racked up an impressive 16 assists. Hector's generous play allowed others like Peter Thomas, the Sanchez brothers, and Christopher Medina to have banner days. St. Michael's blew out Holy Child, 71 – 54. It was the team's first win and they were content.

Hector headed home…

"Yes, the check is here!" Esmeralda cried aloud. She was desperate for cash and she had been waiting for her unemployment checks to begin. The check was not much - $300.00 per week. But, it was enough to pay for the groceries, and if she budgeted properly, she might be able to keep the landlord off her back.

"Mami, we won today!" Hector was proud of himself and he was proud of his teammates. "That is wonderful, *mi amor.*" Hector felt like a good son being able to place a smile on his mother's face. But this happiness was short lived. As the hour faded, Esmeralda began contemplating their financial misfortune. Observing his mother's face turn to a blank stare broke Hector's heart. Hector wished her mother didn't have to struggle and he wished he did not have to struggle too. The unemployment check would have to do; Esmeralda would have to stretch the money as far as possible.

For once, Hector did not have to worry about the money situation at home, but he had other thoughts on his mind. He decided to walk to the library and get a "cheat sheet" for *Romeo and Juliet*. "Maybe…" Hector thought to himself, "If I can get one of those cheat sheet study guides, I won't have to actually read the stupid play." As he was walking to the local library, he noticed the rosary beads were hanging outside of St. Michael's. "I guess the priest is home," Hector thought to himself. He didn't think much of it, but then he noticed the colors of the Snipers. He couldn't make out who they were, but he didn't want to take any chances. He scooted up the church steps and squeezed through the heavy oak doors.

Father Malloy heard the pitter pattering and wet squeaking of sneakers on the marble floors. "Hello?" the cleric questioned to the air. "Hey Father, it's me, Hector." "To what do I owe the honor?" the priest playfully questioned.

"You know, Father Malloy, I'm kinda in trouble in a few ways. I messed up a bit and I owe some people some money - $300.00 bucks. Plus, I'm failing my English class. We're reading some stupid play, *Romeo and Juliet,* and my teacher said that I might get left back."

The priest took a moment to think about how to approach these two unique issues.

"It sounds to me that you are the creator of these problems. The good news is that you are also the solution to each problem.

Correct me if I'm wrong, but it seems as though you put yourself into both of these situation. The good news, however, is that if you can get into something, you can also get out of it."

The priest continued. "Perhaps you could work a few hours extra during the week and pay off the debt you owe."

Hector replied, "I would, but you see, my mom is out of work and anything I get, I give it to her."

"I see…and what about the English class? Are you truly giving it everything you've got?"

"Well, I guess not." Hector began to look at his sneakers and scratch his head.

"I think I can help you, Hector. But you need to agree to work harder at home and in school." Hector nodded his head that he would. "Alright, I have a few ideas. Tell you what, have the team meet me here at the church this Friday at 4:30pm. Don't be late. And dress sharp!"

"Ok, but what for?" Hector was confused. Why did he need the others?

"You'll see."

The week went by, and Hector was able to stay away from the fray of the Snipers. He was able to get the entire team together.

The guys on the team did not know what to expect, but they what they did know was that Father Malloy wanted them together. He truly believed that spending more time with one another made them better basketball players and better teammates. "It adds to our chemistry," Malloy often repeated.

"Hey, Hector, do you know where we're going?" questioned Peter. Chris Medina added to the speculation, "Maybe he's taking us to see the Knicks. That would be the bomb!"

Anticipation grew as Father Malloy met the team inside the church doors. He was dressed in his formal black suit with the Roman white collar cuffed around his neck. The forecasted weather called for freezing winds. The priest took heed to the weather warning as he donned a black wool button down jacket and sported a gray fedora atop his head. "Well, boys, we are going to New York City tonight. I have a friend who owes me a favor and he's agreed to send me tickets to see the famous musical, *West Side Story*."

This news was not met with open arms. "A musical? That's corny. I don't do musicals," Henry Patterson firmly declared. "Yea, Father Malloy, take us somewhere cool, like to a Knicks game or something. Why do we have to go to some silly, girly play?" added a disappointed Chris Medina.

"There's a reason why we must go tonight. First of all, I think you all need some time together where you aren't focusing on basketball. Basketball is a great game. But there is much more to life than sports. It is important to be well-rounded. We all could use some exposure to the arts and to culture. Besides, this play is about two tough gangs from New York City! You're going to love it!"

Gangs? That's the last word Hector wanted to hear. He had been avoiding the Snipers the entire week. It was simply exhausting. He was grateful to get out of Staten Island for one night. Plus, he had never been to a Broadway play before. He often would hear other kids at school talk about Broadway, and he never really knew what they meant. Finally, he would have something to add to that conversation, thanks to the man in black.

The entire team took the city bus to the Staten Island Ferry. They were grumbling a little less than before, as they were enjoying each other's company. There were a few sarcastic remarks made, but Malloy didn't mind being the butt of a few jokes if the end result was improved team harmony. The crisp night air invigorated the boys, and the city looked magnificent against a full moon light. While the ferry was half-way to its destination, every young man leaned up against the left rail of the boat as they silently enjoyed the iconic *Statue of Liberty.* This trip for some, like Jamaal and Christopher, was the first time off the island. It was also their first time to a fancy play.

"Now, remember, you're going into a Broadway theatre. This is not the movies and it is not the playground. The only reason I was able to get these tickets was because one of the lead actors owes me a favor. Be respectful and enjoy the show. Act as if you are in church. I know you will be on your best behavior." The priest was clear of his high expectations.

"Hey, Father, what was the favor you did?" Pablo wondered aloud. "I was the priest who married the actor playing Tony with his wife. His name is Rob Brown. He told me that if I ever needed tickets to see him, that they were mine. So I'm taking him up on his offer."

As the coach and team entered the theatre, the boys felt a bit uncomfortable. They weren't used to well-dressed people, wearing high end suits and extravagant dresses drinking expensive cocktails. Father Malloy did not have enough money to buy overly expensive food and beverage at the theatre so he told the boys that they would eat after the show.

In the opening scene of the play, a white teenage gang and a Puerto Rican teenage gang break out in a street fight. Malloy glanced at his team and their eyes were as wide as silver dollar pancakes. He knew he had them in the palm of his hand. The glorious music and cultural dance only intensified the boys' appetite for more.

Malloy kept a close eye on Hector. He could see Hector beginning to put two-and-two together. *Two gangs who disliked one another – just like two households. A forbidden love – Maria and Tony, just like Romeo and Juliet. Both guys do not want to fight, but are forced to. The great plan does not go as expected. The gangs, just like the Montagues and Capulets, will not let them be together.* Hector's mouth was open and his face looked as if he was having an epiphany. Hector turned his head to look at the priest who was sitting at the end of the row. Father Malloy was nodding his head to Hector, knowing exactly what he was thinking. *This story was the same as Romeo and Juliet. Maybe "Romeo and Juliet" isn't so bad after all?* Hector decided then and there that it was time to stop running away from his problems and to start giving his school work his all. He was truly impressed and humbled that his coach, the Priest, would go to such great lengths in order to help him pass a class.

The boys were better than their word and behaved with great maturity. Afterwards, Malloy took them to a local pizza joint where they discussed the play. Mario Sanchez led off, "Yo, that guy Bernardo was awesome! He was tough, just like me." "Ummmm...yea, just like you," Jamaal sarcastically retorted. Then, Mickey Sullivan feigned a punch to Mario's face and Mario flinched. "You're a real hero, Mario or should I say, Maria!" They all had a great laugh and were having a grand time. "Hey Father Malloy, what was your favorite part of the play?" Joseph Tucker questioned the wise elder of the group.

The team was curious as to what Father Malloy thought because the play had plenty of drama. "Well, the story is indeed a tragedy. There are many exciting scenes, but I really enjoy the dancing. I am partial to the scene when both gangs dance the competition mambo dance. That scene is done with great precision and the music is fabulous. I love how the dance reveals the differences within the American and Puerto Rican culture." They boys were cool with fact that Malloy respected the arts.

Father Malloy wanted to make sure that the boys understood the message of the play. "However, if you ask me which scene is the most important, to me, it is when the Sharks and Jets agree to end the feud. It is symbolic of how in America, people of various cultures have to learn to live with each other. Look at us; we are all different. If you take each player's talent, however, and use it correctly, the team becomes a glorious mosaic of cultures and abilities."

This seemed to pump up the entire team and they went home ready to tackle their next opponent.

Game 4: St. Adalbert's vs. St. Michael's

The second home game was finally at hand. The team was fresh off their first victory and their bonding experience. While the guys didn't get home until 11:30 pm, they still were running smoothly. The chemistry was growing and a mediocre St. Adalbert's team was not going to stop this emerging giant. Peter Thomas demonstrated a great deal of progress. His ball handling skills were improving, as he did not have one turnover the entire game. He was certainly growing into a strong reserve role player for Fr. Malloy. This allowed Malloy to tinker with the lineup.

For example, the padre at times, played Hector alongside Peter. Since Peter was able to move the ball so well, it opened up Hector to hit some mid range jumpers. This took a lot of pressure off Hector as the team now found other ways to score points. Just like the young buck, this team was digging their legs into the tundra. As for the other players, the big men had a great day rebounding. St. Michael's out-rebounded the opposition 45 boards to 29. This led to many second chance points. It was certain that St. Michael's was the more talented team and the coach was inspiring the team to reach new heights. The final score was St. Michael's 72 – St. Adalbert's 61. Father Malloy was enthralled that the team was now at 2-2, gaining momentum with each and every day.

Chapter 11:

"What you get by achieving your goals is not as important as what you become by achieving your goals."

– Henry David Thoreau

Sunday Mass – 10:30 am.

Father Malloy awoke with cold and fresh November air entering his lungs. He accidentally left his window open the night before. There was an empty red wine bottle sitting on his night stand next to a scarlet ringed drinking glass. Perhaps the good friar had too much celebration the night prior. Regardless, he emerged energetic ready to tackle the morning masses.

Once again, his team attended the mass, but this time Hector came along too. He was accompanied by his mother, who sat a few rows behind Hector. Hector's mom was proud to see that he was a part of a team. All of the boys looked so handsome, she thought to herself.

Father Malloy knew he was making strides with the boys and with the congregation. He leaned on a famous prayer entitled, *Footprints* to help get his message across.

"One night I dreamed I was walking along the beach with the Lord.
Many scenes from my life flashed across the sky.
In each scene I noticed footprints in the sand.
Sometimes there were two sets of footprints.
Other times there were one set of footprints.

*This bothered me because I noticed that during the low periods
of my life
When I was suffering from anguish, sorrow, or defeat,
I could see only one set of footprints.
So I said to the Lord, "You promised me, Lord,
That if I followed you, you would walk with me always.
But I noticed that during the most trying periods of my life
There have only been one set of prints in the sand.
Why, When I have needed you most, you have not been there for
me?"
The Lord replied,
"The times when you have seen only one set of footprints
Is when I carried you."*

Father Malloy hoped that the famous prayer would stay with the boys. One day, he would not be there to guide them. They would need to rely on God and each other. That moment would come sooner than the priest thought.

After Fr. Malloy completed mass, Hector's mother pitter pattered her feet toward the priest, excited to finally speak to him. The conservatively dressed mother spoke to the priest in broken English.

"*Dios Mio! Gracias*, Father Malloy for all of your help. I notice a change in my boy. My Hector is trying hard in school and he talks about the team all the time. Gracias, Padre Malloy!"

"*No problema, Senora Ruiz. Su muchacho juega con mucho corazon!* He plays with heart and courage. He is a *leon* or a lion on the court. It has been an honor to work with him.

Hector's mouth hit the church floor as he realized the priest could speak Spanish fluently. Hector started to rack his brain thinking of all the times he had cursed at the priest in his native tongue.

"Father Malloy, why didn't you tell me you knew Spanish?" Hector was standing in amazement with his hands resting on his hips. Unbeknownst to Hector, Father Malloy was well versed in the Spanish language. The priest had learned Spanish fluently while serving as a chaplain for the United States Army base in Honduras. Honduras, located in Central America, provided Malloy with an opportunity to work on his Spanish and to serve the faithful on and off the base.

"You never asked!- *Tu nunca preguntaste.*" The mother began laughing and she and the priest enjoyed more pleasantries. It gave Malloy great joy to see Hector's mother filled with joy and enthusiasm. These were the moments Malloy lived for. It was why he wanted to join the priesthood, to help others.

It seemed as though Father Malloy was truly helping the people of St. Michael's. His flock was growing and thriving. It had been a long time for Port Richmond to cheer for a church, a team, a priest.

Father Malloy's success did not go unnoticed. The person responsible for placing Malloy at St. Michael's was quite aware of Malloy's efforts. Cardinal John McNamara was known as the "Cardinal of the City" and was of course, a member of the College of Cardinals who eventually would decide on future popes.

Cardinal McNamara knew he had someone of great talent on his hands. Father Malloy, in his prior stint at St. Helen's in Woodhaven, Queens, was able to raise over $70,000 dollars in order to purchase a new roof and install new basketball hoops for their gymnasium. Now, it was only a matter of time before he would place his new rising star in a more permanent position.

Recently, there was an opening at St. Patrick's Cathedral in Manhattan, New York. St. Patrick's Cathedral was the Carnegie Hall of all churches. A monsignor had unexpectedly retired and left a gaping hole in the famous cathedral's hierarch. The available position was entitled, *Ambassador to Vatican City*. This meant that the priest would be responsible for all communications with Rome. This person would be the lead dog in all foreign affairs. This meant rubbing elbows with bishops, the cardinal and of course, the pope. It was a position to die for. Cardinal McNamara had only one "man in black" in mind.

The Cardinal decided to officially offer the good priest the position by writing a letter by hand. Even in an ever changing world, the church still honored time honored traditions. The Cardinal's message was as follows:

Attention: Father James Malloy

Greetings! I have been reviewing your work at St. Michael's Roman Catholic Church and I am quite satisfied. You have once again, exceeded your duties. You have certainly demonstrated yourself capable of greater responsibilities. Therefore, you will be leaving St. Michael's and taking a new position as Ambassador to Vatican City no later than January 1, 2013. Should you have any questions, feel free to contact me. Once again, you have done a marvelous job at your new parish.

In Christ Jesus,

Cardinal John McNamara

The letter was sent with little delay and the news would leave Malloy in a quandary.

Practice – Monday, November 18, 2013

Fr. Malloy was running his team pretty hard to start the practice. While the players were now buying in, he needed them to know they hadn't achieved anything yet.

When coaches are asked about why they lost a close game, they sometimes remark about a play here or there. It is actually the little things that we can do on the court that separates winning from losing. For example, when there's a loose ball on the court, who wants it more? When a teammate goes sprawling on the floor, how many teammates are there to pick him up? When a player makes a poor pass or takes a poor shot, do you remind that player that he is a good player? Or do you snicker to yourself remarking on his faults? We need to grab that extra rebound, dive for that extra inch, and extend our hands just a little bit further.

After practice, Alice handed the priest the day's mail. One in particular looked important. It was from St. Patrick's Cathedral. When Malloy realized that this was a hand written letter from Cardinal McNamara himself, the priest quickly excused himself from Alice to more secluded quarters.

"Bless my soul, working at THE St. Patrick's Cathedral." Malloy pondered his future with great delight for he was keenly aware that this offer was as remarkable as it was rare. A feeling of guilt then began to emerge as the faces of the boys began clouding his mind. Slowly, each player on the team, his face was like a slot machine, and instead of lucky sevens spinning around, it was the faces of the boys of St. Michael's. The priest was befuddled. He walked over to his book case and picked up an old tennis ball he used to use when he played stickball. He lay in his bed with the ball in his hand. He began throwing the ball up and playing catch with it. He needed time to think.

Whichever decision he made, he would win, but he would also lose.

Game 5: St. Claire's vs. St. Michael's

This game began inauspiciously for St. Michael's. The center for St. Claire's was manhandling Jamaal and Henry. His name was Luke Jospey, and he was a beast. His thighs and calves were as thick as an oak tree. When his rugged, muscular arms were extended during a box out, the rebound was his. He was getting garbage put backs, and providing second chance scoring for his team. This was going to be a good test for Malloy's boys. After the first quarter, St. Michael's was trailing by nine points. At the end of the first quarter, Malloy wanted to break out his full-court press.

"Now boys, listen up. Just like we talked about during practice; Stay in front of the ball, move with your offensive player. If you beat him to the spot, we will win this game! Don't begin the press right out of the time out. Wait until after their first possession. This way, the full court press will come as a surprise. Remember, play together!"

After the opposing team's first possession, Malloy's team turned up the heat on defense. Of course, their defensive champion, Christopher Medina led the charge. Watching Christopher was like watching a mind reader at work as he continually beat his offensive counterpart to the desired spot. He was personally responsible for creating seven turnovers in twelve trips down the floor. Christopher had four steals himself. The rest of the players followed suit. Hector was able to team up with Christopher and collapse on the St. Claire point guard. The guard picked up his dribble before half court and was called for a

10 seconds violation. The second quarter belonged to St. Michael's as they stormed back to take the lead 42 – 39.

During halftime, the priest made some adjustments to defending Luke Jospey. He decided to "front the player" which meant that he would stick a big forward like Jamaal in front of Luke at all times. While this would open up a weakness under the hoop, Malloy knew that their guards weren't talented enough to put enough touch on the passes.

As predicted, the priest's strategy was correct. The team surged ahead. Malloy figured today was as good as any other day to plan for the future. "Joseph, come here. I want you to coach the fourth quarter. You know our team better than anyone. You can do it."

There was a large lump in Tucker's throat as he nervously grabbed the clipboard with the opposing roster. Father Malloy called time out to inform the team. "Ok boys, Joseph is going to lead us the rest of the way. He has scouted the other team. He knows their weaknesses and he knows your strengths. Joseph, the team's yours."

Some of the boys, like Peter and Jamaal raised an eyebrow. But, Hector began clapping his hands. He looked at Tucker straight in the eye, and said, "Ok coach, what should we do next?" Tucker could see that Hector was taking a leap of faith in following Tucker. Hector knew if he didn't' believe in Joseph Tucker, the rest of the team would rip at the seams.

Seeing that the rest of the team followed Hector's cue, Joseph drew up a play. "Listen to me, their best strength can be turned into a weakness. They are great at rebounding down low, but they can't stop open three point shots. So, this is what we're going to do. We're going to go with a small lineup and spread them out. I want Hector at the point, with Sully at shooting guard. Then, I need Christopher Medina at the shooting guard spot. Mario, you go in for Henry. And Jamaal, you're going to clog up that big goon down low. Hector, drive and dish…drive and dish! You guys got it!"

They all obliged.

This formula was met with a handshake from Fr. Malloy and it actually worked. The Malloy boys were raining threes from all over the court. Even though the other team had big rebounders, the long shots resulted in scores or long rebounds which the quicker guards like Medina gobbled up. Game over.

St. Michael's 78 – St. Claire's 70.

"Hey, let's go celebrate!" Jamaal exclaimed. "Yea, let's go to that diner on Port Richmond Avenue," chimed in Pablo. Hector nodded his head in agreement. Unfortunately, this wasn't a home game, so they had to take two city buses to get back to Port Richmond. The rest of the guys weren't up for that mission so they declined the offer. Father Malloy offered to drive the boys, but once they heard they would have to make a pit stop at another church, they said *thanks but no thanks.*

The three teammates took the first city bus, got a transfer to the #44 bus and completed the ride to Port Richmond Avenue. Walking together, they began to talk about the game. "Yo, Hector, you broke that kid's ankles when you crossed him over," said Jamal. "Yea, you were a beast out there," added Pablo. "Thanks guys, you guys were good, too!" Their warm moment was short lived as they turned the corner. It was Terry and three other Snipers. Hector had managed to clude the gang for weeks but now it was time to pay the piper. Terry wasn't going to let a perfect opportunity like this pass him by. Instantly, he grabbed

Hector by both hands. Terry seemed to be twice his size. Jamaal and Pablo were held back by the other gang members. "Look what the lawnmower dragged in. Where's my money, punk!" There was silence for a moment, and then Terry punched Hector in the face. Hector winced in pain. Jamaal and Pablo were in shock. They had no idea Hector was involved with the gang. Though in shock, Pablo felt that Terry was going overboard with Hector. He also felt Terry was throwing racial slurs around, Pablo was Mexican too. Gathering all of his courage, he pushed away the Sniper who was holding him, ran into Terry and threw his shoulder into his stomach. This knocked Terry to the ground. "C'mon...Vamonos! Let's get out of here!" cried Pablo. The three players began running from the gang and were making their way towards the church until they heard a heart-stopping sound. "BANG!" A single shot was fired and smoke was exiting a revolver which was held by the leader of the Snipers.

Jamaal kept running until he heard his own name screamed out in a desperate voice. "Jamaal, help!" Lying helplessly on the sidewalk was Pablo. He had been struck by the gang leader's bullet. The bullet had pierced Pablo's upper right leg and he was crying out in agony. Terry heard the voice too, and was closing in to end the job. Instantly, the rhythmic sound of sirens echoed through the street. It was a marked NYPD police car streaking down the street. Terry backed away from Pablo and took off with the Snipers; they all vanished without a trace.

The police surveyed the scene, treated Pablo for potential shock and called an ambulance. Two officers took Jamaal and Hector in for questioning. On the way to the police station, Jamaal called Father Malloy and told the priest about Pablo. Father Malloy quickly changed from his comfortable clothes into his "priest gear" and headed for the hospital. Father Malloy was breathing heavily and his stomach was in knots. He combated his wild imagination with prayer and positive thinking. *"Lord above, please give strength to one of my players, Pablo Sanchez. May he remain healthy and recover quickly."*

Father Malloy arrived at Staten Island Hospital and rushed to the emergency room. The white walls of the emergency room sent chills down the priest's spine as he had visited this place often. Sometimes he had to give last rites to a dying man or woman, other times he had to console families of the deceased. Malloy thought of Pablo and his brother, Mario. He saw Mario with his mother in the waiting room. He greeted them with warm embraces and said a prayer for Pablo. Even while in prayer, Father Malloy was thinking other thoughts. *How could this happen?* He even began to blame himself. *I should have stayed with them!* After hearing more details about the events that transpired, Father Malloy knew the Snipers were the culprits.

Pulling Hector to the side, the priest questioned the teen. "Hector, tell me the truth. What happened exactly?" Father Malloy demanded honesty in this situation. Hector didn't want to talk. He grew aggravated with the point guard so he moved on to Jamaal. "Jamaal, tell me right now how this happened!" Malloy could tell that he didn't want to be known as a snitch. "Jamaal, don't forget, I'm a priest. Whatever you say to me is in confidence." This put Jamaal at ease as he was looking for a reason to talk to the priest. "It's Hector. He owes the Snipers money. Pablo tried to get Hector, and me out of the there, but that kid Terry was carrying a gun. He shot him as we ran away."

Father Malloy grinded his teeth as he became visibly angry. He thanked Jamaal for telling him the truth, but deep down an overwhelming feeling of vengeance and rage burned.

He was also furious with Hector for getting involved with a terrible crowd and for putting innocent people in harm's way. Malloy made sure to go back to Hector. He pulled him to the side. "Why do you owe the Snipers money? How could you put Pablo's, Jamaal's, and your own life in jeopardy?"

"I needed the money. My mom ain't working. We don't have any food, man!"

Malloy was bewildered at Hector's selfish and careless behavior, but he decided it was more important to hold his tongue and find out as much information as possible. The priest needed to know the truth. "How much do you owe?"

"Over 300 dollars," replied a forthright Hector. "By accident, I robbed a member of the Snipers. I know I messed up. I'm gonna get the money."

"No one accidentally robs anyone! Hector, I'm extremely disappointed in you." This statement cut like a knife. Hector knew he was beginning to gain Father Malloy's trust, and losing that was a difficult pill to swallow. Father Malloy told Hector that he should have went to him about his family situation. He also explained to Hector that his family's issues do not excuse the act of stealing money. "You and Jamaal make sure you get the team here tomorrow at noon. That's an order!" Malloy wanted to make sure that Pablo knew he had the support of the entire team in this difficult time.

Luckily for Pablo, his injury was not life threatening. However, that would be the last organized basketball game he would ever play in. The ligaments in his legs were severed and his thigh muscles were shredded by the bullet. It would take almost a year before Pablo could walk without crutches. He would always walk with a slight limp for the rest of his life.

The next day, the team came to visit Pablo in the hospital. Pablo's leg was hurting him greatly, but not being able to play on the team was his core source of pain. "I can't believe this happened! No more basketball? I'm going to miss being on the team." Father Malloy stepped forward, "Are you kidding me? You're still on the team. And you will walk soon enough. I know it!" Mario tried to lighten the mood. "Yea, for now you're the water boy." A smile finally emerged on Pablo's face and it warmed his heart to know that he was a part of a team who cared for him.

The team visited Pablo for a few hours. They talked about school, who-was-dating-who, the newest horror film that was out, and about girls again. During these moments, Father Malloy rolled his eyes or pretended to cough with the purpose of reminding the boys they were standing in front of a *man of the cloth.* "Boys will be boys," Father Malloy muttered. Henry and Mickey patted the priest on the back and the atmosphere of the room was becoming increasingly playful.

It was seemingly almost a party before Pablo made one final request before the team left. "There's only one thing I want from you all. And that's to win it all! Everything we worked for this year will be for nothing if we can't finish the job. We didn't run a million wind sprints and suicides to lose now!"

The entire team began to clap in unison around Pablo. Malloy scanned the room and what he saw was a true team.

The team held their end of the bargain as they continued to win. They won the next four games by double-digit points. They defeated St. Rita's, Blessed Sacrament, Holy Cross, and St. Sylvester's respectively. This new streak catapulted St.

Michael's into third place with a 7 – 2 record. The playoffs were around the corner. The team was still managing to play well, but the Snipers still lurked in the shadows. When the detectives interviewed Hector, Jamaal and Pablo, they all said that they couldn't identify the shooter. The three of them knew all too well that if you snitched on a Sniper, you and your family would be subject to an attack. They couldn't risk the Snipers coming after their families in the middle of the night. So, for the time being, they remained quiet. They hoped that somehow the police would nab Terry in another fashion.

The boys, instead, focused their energy on getting ready for the playoffs. Their next game was the last for the regular season.

Chapter 12:

"You wouldn't have won if we'd beaten you."

– *Yogi Berra*

Game 10: St. Andrew's vs. St. Michael's

There was an eerie vibe in the freezing December air as Malloy entered the gym. He wasn't feeling well; he was suffering from a 101 degree fever. Despite his own ailments, he was determined to lead his team to a win so as to build even more momentum for the playoffs.

The opposing team, St. Andrew's, had a strong record themselves. At 5 - 4, the team was having a respectable run. This game was especially important to St. Andrew's because a win would lock up a playoff spot. There were six teams invited to the playoffs and a win would lock them into the final sixth seed. If they lost the game, they would have to get help from other teams in order to make it into the tournament.

Father Malloy took a knee and explained to the players to work on their fundamentals and to continue to trust each other. He sent out Hector at the point, Sully at the shooting guard spot, Medina was at the three, followed by Jamaal at power forward, and Patterson at center.

At the outset, the team was not jiving together. Hector turned the ball over three times in seven possessions leading to eight uncontested points. It wasn't only Hector who was struggling. Mickey Sullivan had gone cold from long range. And it wasn't only the fact that he went cold, he seemed to be getting lazy with his form and he wasn't interested in going after long rebounds.

On two occasions, Mickey's shot hit the back of the rim sending the ball deep. If Sullivan had gone after the rebound with authority, he would have secured two extra possessions.

Jamaal was getting rebounds, but he wasn't getting enough elevation on his jump shot and was blocked on several attempts. To make matters worse, the team was complaining to the referees about foul calls and Henry earned himself a technical foul for slamming the ball down in frustration. *Where are our heads?* Father Malloy began to wonder.

Father Malloy called timeout in the second quarter. He decided to make some changes. He sent in Peter Thomas and Mario Sanchez in order to enhance the ball handling and quickness. But it was of no use. The team was getting run up and down the court by St. Andrew's. The opposing point guard, Jeremy Wallace, was a skinny and frail looking player, but boy could he run. He sped past the entire defense; even Hector could not keep up with him. This game was over before it started. Final score: St. Andrew's 76 – St. Michael's 61.

Father Malloy congratulated the opposing coach and his players. He also made sure that his own players demonstrated good sportsmanship by watching them shake the other team's hands.

The loss dropped St. Michael's into the fourth seed of an eight team playoff. The top two seeds, Our Lady of Pity and St. Patrick's, were quite formidable. St. Michael's was bunched up with a few other solid teams. The playoff rankings are as follows:

#1 – Our Lady of Pity – record: 10 – 0.

#2 – St. Patrick's – record – 9 -1.

#3 – Queen of Peace – record – 7 - 3.

\#4 – St. Michael's – record 7 – 3.

\#5 – St. Andrew's – record – 6 – 4.

\#6 – St. Adalbert's –record 6- 4.

\#7 – Holy Family – record 5 – 5.

\#8 – Holy Child – record 5 – 5.

The first round match ups were as follows:

(1) Our Lady of Pity vs. (8) Holy Child
(2) St. Patrick's vs.(7) Holy Family
(3) Queen of Peace vs. (6) St. Adalbert's
(4) St. Michael's vs. (5) St. Andrew's

Practice –

The team was out of sync. Father Malloy needed to think of a way to get them back on track. He knew they could shoot, pass, rebound and do all the physical things it takes to win basketball games. They had grown complacent and they needed a wake-up call. So Father Malloy did something quite peculiar. Instead on working a new play or fundamentals, he took them to a professional basketball game. Father Malloy managed to secure the nose-bleed seats in Madison Square Garden in order to watch the New York Knicks. They were having a successful campaign this year and the boys were excited and grateful to be able to go. Just like the Broadway play, it would be the first time the players watched professionals play the game they all loved.

At the game, every Malloy boy was well behaved. Mario and his teammates took turns pushing Pablo in his wheel chair. One unintended perk was the fact that they were so high up in the arena, the coach was able to speak to them all without disturbing other fans. Father Malloy would say things like, "Did you see how the point guard lulled his defended to sleep and then exploded to the hoop?" or he would say, "Did you notice how the low post defenders come to each other's aid?" The boys were once again perplexed by Malloy's attention to detail. It seemed as though Malloy wanted the boys to scout the Knicks team as much as enjoy the experience for what it was- a night out with family.

In Malloy's opinion, he had done all he could. They knew each other inside and out. They knew what to do. The only question was whether or not they would all come together at the right time.

Playoff Game - St. Michael's vs. St. Andrew's

Father Malloy saw St. Andrew's as a perfect first round match up. Yes, they did just lose to this team, but in Malloy's mind it was due to a lack of hustle and attention to detail than to talent. Father Malloy's message to his team was clear. He gathered them together and took a knee.

"It has been my privilege to be your coach. Now, our season does not have to end today. It does not have to end today because you will listen to each other and work as one fine oiled-machine. When you do, there is no team on God's green earth that can stop you. Now let's take care of business!"

This invigorated an already refocused bunch. Fr. Malloy went with his small lineup because ball handling was an issue in the prior match. So he sent out Peter Thomas to team with Hector in the back court, while Christopher would hold down the small forward position, Mickey Sullivan was almost like a second small forward with Jamaal situated at center.

Both teams started off a little sluggish. And then Fr. Malloy put on a full court press. He had his fastest defenders on the court and he decided it was the perfect moment to attack. Once again, Malloy was pressing all the right buttons. Medina and Peter twice stole the ball and were able to lead multiple fast court breaks. St. Michael's was scoring baskets in transition. Hector was working well with Jamaal in the pick-and-roll game. Hector was splitting the defense and either scoring himself or sending the ball to open teammates. One teammate in particular, Mickey Sullivan, hit back to back three-pointers in the outset of the second quarter. The team was outplaying St. Andrew's in every facet. St. Andrew's was able to mount a respectable comeback in the second half, but it was not enough. St. Michael's won fairly easily and the boys were surprised how much better they were this week than the one prior. It was on to the semifinals as they awaited the winner of the matchup between St. Patrick's and Holy Family.

The results of the other games were announced via Staten Island Sound radio station or *SIS station.* They announced at 6:00 pm the results of the first round matches.

Our Lady of Pity – 78   Holy Child - 56

St. Patrick's – 78 – Holy Family - 60

St. Adalbert's 54 – Queen of Peace 52

St. Michael's 68 – St. Andrew's 59

The results of the first round games went as expected with the higher seeds winning out, however, St. Adalbert's shocked the CYO league by defeating Queen of Peace. For Father Malloy and St. Michael's, this meant they had to face the supremely talented St. Patrick's in the semifinal round.

Chapter 13:

"The family is one of nature's masterpieces."

– George Santayana

Sunday, December 17

Father Malloy spent the week tweaking the decorations for the holiday season. Malloy loved the Nativity scene of Mary, Joseph and the Baby Jesus. In a separate prayer room in the back of the church, Father Malloy set up hand-carved Nativity sets that he collected from around the world. Some sets were collected on Malloy's visits, others he was given as gifts. There was a chiseled crystal Nativity set from Ireland and a carved wooden one from Mexico. There was an ivory Nativity imported from Africa and several others set up in the room. The room was often filled with people admiring the Holy Family from around the globe.

Father Malloy wanted to focus on three of his own personal heroes of the Bible. With a humble demeanor, Father Malloy began to speak from the pulpit. He decided to use his personal heroes of the Bible; the Magi.

"Today's message is about Melchior, Caspar and Balthazar, otherwise known as the three wise men."

"Upon calculating the stars, the Magi made their way to see the new born King. However, this journey was not without danger. The Roman Emperor heard of this "new king prophesy" and told these Magi to inform him of the Savior's whereabouts. After greeting the Baby Jesus and presenting him with gifts of gold, frankincense and myrrh, they left and traveled another way so as

to avoid the Roman Emperor. It took great courage to stick together and it took steady faith to place their fates in the hands of the Lord. The wise men were heroic. The three men were sustained by faith in each other and faith in the Lord. As we are coming close to Christmas, let's remember in our hearts that it is our faith that binds us all."

The team was listening attentively and couldn't help but think Father Malloy was speaking only to them. Father Malloy hoped that the courage displayed by the wise men could somehow transfer into his own players.

Father Malloy was greeted, yet again, warmly by his humble homily. Even though it was the holiday season, the priest was secretly yearning for church services to end. Malloy was craving free time. He could not wait to get back to the rectory where he could listen to the tape recorded playoff game between St. Patrick's and Holy Family. The Staten Island local radio station aired all the C.Y.O. games, and Malloy recorded it. Radio was old fashioned, but it worked just fine for the resourceful coach.

Malloy put on a pot of coffee, added some sugar and milk and settled into his living room chair. He listened carefully. He would need to find a weakness in the opposition to offset the blowout loss earlier in the year.

As the announcers foretold the game, it sounded like St. Patrick's was a strong all around team. "Good point guard....good center," Malloy thought to himself. "Where can it be? It must be somewhere...No team is perfect!" Malloy was determined to find a chink in the armor. Finally, a thought entered his mind. He wasn't sure if his theory would hold water. He needed to listen to the complete game. As the fourth quarter played itself out, Malloy started to smile to himself. The coach finally found something to zoom in on in practice. The announcers only announced two substitutions for the entire game for St. Patrick's. This was extremely rare in CYO basketball. Father Malloy was able to draw two conclusions based on this fact. "St. Patrick's does not have depth, and they are not comfortable going deep into their bench." This was a marvelous find for the priest because this meant that if forced to go to their bench, St. Patrick's players would neither have the familiarity or confidence to play with the unit out on the court. Therefore, Father Malloy's new goal was to get into the paint and get their best players in foul trouble.

Monday Practice

Father Malloy went for a morning run. It was brutally cold, but the sun was out and if dressed appropriately, the weather was not too much of a discomfort. He was energized by his research and he was also excited to teach the boys something new. He had something up his sleeve.

Mickey Sullivan arrived early as usual. He asked Father Malloy if he thought they had a good chance this coming weekend. "Of course, we do. They're probably asking their coach the same question." Mickey nodded his head and smirked. But, Malloy could tell confidence was going to be an issue today. He realized that the last time they played St. Patrick's; they had virtually been blown out. He was going to have to pull out all the stops if he was going to convince the group they were capable of winning.

All the boys arrived and began performing their warm up stretches. "Father Malloy, we won last week. But, this week we have to go vs. St. Pats. They're like basically undefeated," Joseph Tucker wanted to hear something positive from the coach.

"Well, I'm not going to lie to you boys, it's going to be a tough game. But, it is one we can win. Now, I had a feeling you all were going to be sharing some of these thoughts. That's why I brought something to show you."

Malloy brought out a 20" television that was resting on a square stand that had four wheels on the bottom of each corner. The television was then pushed to right underneath the basketball hoop. He asked that the entire team take a knee by the foul line.

"I'm going to show you something that you need to see. Many of you think that just because we lost by double digits last time, that we are destined to lose again. However, this is not the case. All we need is some confidence. Now, watch this film clip I found on a nature program."

"Nature program? What are you gonna show us – elephants shooting three pointers?" joked Mario. Fr. Malloy was expecting a sarcastic response, so he had one in return. "If I had an elephant that hit three pointers, I wouldn't need any of you."

The film clip began. The setting of the video clip was an African jungle. At the outset, an entire lion pride, maybe 10 to 12 lions, were all sharing in a kill of two zebras. Then, something incredible happened. The camera then focused on three African men who were wearing robes. These men were extremely thin, maybe 120 pounds each. One male lion could kill all three in a few minutes. However, these men were not scared of this lion pride. The three men walked in unison, but they didn't actually walk, they marched together. They were marching directly toward the lion pride.

At this point, the boys were going bonkers. "Are these guys' nuts?" Jamaal announced. "Oh my God, these guys are gonna get eaten," declared Peter.

"Shh! Now, watch what they do next," ordered the priest.

The three men increased their pace marching right into the lion pride. This extremely brash and strange behavior startled the entire pride. Every single member of the pride began to disperse in panic. The pride hid behind rocks and trees while the three African men took bones and pieces of meat that they would later use to feed their families. Being of small stature, they could only carry so much meat. As soon as they took a few hunks for themselves, they were off to their village. They did not waver. They did not quiver. They did not look behind them. They simply walked back home. Only when the coast was clear, did those mighty lions return to their feast.

The priest let the video sit with the boys for a good two minutes. "Now, what was the point of that video?"

"Uh…don't go to Africa," declared Mickey Sullivan. "Hey, my grandmother is from Kenya!" Henry was wearing a "fake-serious" face when he questioned Mickey. Father Malloy interjected, "Can someone here please explain this video?"

Jamaal stood up and announced, "Father Malloy, it means we gotta have confidence. We gotta show no fear."

"That's exactly right!" Father Malloy excitedly declared. "Just because you lost before does not mean you will lose again. As a matter of fact, I'm not planning on losing for the rest of the year."

This seemed to lift the spirits of everyone. They enthusiastically began practicing working on their traditional plays, but also something new. They worked on driving to the hoop with authority. They also practiced their post moves with the focal point on getting as close to the rim as possible. Malloy knew that some shots would be blocked, but the ones that were unblocked would either going to go in or the other team would get whistled for a foul. The practiced was highly energetic and productive. "They're as ready as they'll ever be," Malloy thought to himself.

Semifinals – St. Michael's vs. St. Patrick's

Once again, St. Patrick's was decked out in brilliant emerald green jerseys with white trim. They were a very strong team. They looked the part and they acted the part. There was a reason why they were 9 – 1 on the year. It was going to take a herculean effort on the part of St. Michael's to overtake them.

Father Malloy asked the boys to kneel before him before tipoff. He led the team in a Hail Mary. "Hail Mary, full of grace, the Lord is with Thee." The boys were locked arm in arm and Malloy was proud. When he saw the solidarity and focus to one common goal, he already knew he won the game. He just didn't tell anyone else.

He sent out his traditional lineup – sending Peter Thomas back to the bench in favor of Henry Patterson. Patterson would be a good rebounder and a strong second option in the post.

At the tip off, the teams began at a frenetic pace. Hector took the team down and broke down a defender and banked a shot off the back board for two points. Then, St. Patrick's best player, Antonio DeShields, hit a 12 foot pull up jumper. This scoring was going back and forth. The defenses of both teams could not slow down anyone. The two teams scored their highest point total in the first quarter, scoring 31 points each. Father Malloy's game plan was working offensively, but he hadn't really made any damage in the foul trouble department.

As both teams headed to their respective benches, Father Malloy implored the team to continue to drive to the paint. He was certain his game plan would work in the end. Because the team ran so hard the first period, Father substituted similar players for similar players. For example, he traded out a solid outside shooter like Mickey for Mario. And then, he substituted Peter Thomas for Christopher Medina. With moves like this, Father Malloy knew his team would be fresher for the fourth quarter. Even though St. Patrick's might be slightly more talented, they just had to wear down eventually.

That time was not coming any time soon, as St. Patrick's went on an 8 – 0 run. DeShields led the charge as he drove the lane and put a spin move on Henry Patterson that perplexed the strong defender. He glided to the hoop and scored with relative ease. He strutted back to the bench as Fr. Malloy called timeout.

"Ok boys, this is where the going gets tough. We're in a hole, so let's stop digging and making matters worse. Now, here's what we're going to do. We're going to double-team DeShields. This team revolves around one player and one player alone. We are a team of players who win together. Now let's make this team earn their points."

The boys went back on the court and continued to drive. Finally, they earned a foul call on DeShields. They worked the ball around and Hector finally found an open Mario Sanchez, who hit a three pointer to cut the deficit to five points. Then on defense, Christopher Medina came to Sullivan's aid and DeShields was forced to give the ball up. The shooting guard took and missed an open shot. "Just as I thought," Malloy figured. Pretty soon, St. Patrick's was missing shots. They were now out of sync as

114

their best player was being harassed mercilessly. St. Patrick's might be the prettiest one-engine plane in the game, but Father Malloy knew he had freight trains ready to barrow down any road.

At half-time, the score was St. Patrick's 62 – St. Michael's 59.

Father Malloy's half time speech was more about the team's destiny than strategic plans.

"We have all come such a long way from the beginning of the season. You are a better team, but more importantly, you are better people. We are united as one and we will take the floor as one. Whatever the outcome, this team has proven itself and has earned my respect. Now, we know what we need to do. Let's go out there and take this win from them. They think they have it, but they don't. They think you'll wilt, but you won't. They think you'll give in because you should, but you won't. We will not stop and we will not give in. Let's go!"

As the third quarter arrived, Father Malloy knew it was going to come down to the wire. He had a feeling he was going to need a surprise performance. Father Malloy never expected this, but Mario Sanchez had the second half of a lifetime. Mario was inspired and focused by the priest's speech, but also because of his injured brother. Mario had extra pep in his step as he quickly curled around screens and knocked down jumpers. He stole the ball from two offensive players and scored on two uncontested layups. He also added a three pointer just before the end of the quarter. In the third quarter, St. Patrick's scored 18 points and Mario scored 16 alone. It was just the push Malloy had been hoping for. DeShields also picked up his second and third personal foul. This also kept the frenetic St. Patrick scoring at bay. At the end of the third quarter, St. Michael's pulled ahead 84 – 80.

The fourth quarter was a brutal affair. Back and forth the teams went. This time, St. Patrick's found their second wind. The guards were hitting their open jumpers and their big men were ripping down rebounds. St. Michael's was hanging on by a thread. With 28 seconds to play, St. Michael's was hanging on to a one point lead. St. Patrick's called timeout. Their coach sketched out a play with DeShields as the focal point. "If we're to go down, we want the ball in Antonio's hands," declared the coach. At the other bench, Father Malloy stressed honoring your zone.

Radio announcer: *"28 seconds to play. The point guard, Denny O'Leary, inbounds the ball to DeShields. DeShields is dribbling the ball through his legs, staring at St. Andrew's best defender, Christopher Medina. DeShields fakes left, now fakes right! Medina is staying right with him. 16 seconds left to play. DeShields drives the lane, gets a step on Medina. He pump fakes a pass to the corner; Patterson buys the fake. DeShields has an open lane. He lays it up and scores with 10 seconds left to play.*

Father Malloy calls his last timeout!"

Father Malloy diagramed the final play. He decided to put the team's fate in the hands of Hector Ruiz. This would be the ultimate sign of faith. The play had several variables, but each variable was dependent upon Hector to control the ball. The way Fr. Malloy envisioned it, Hector would have three options: a) drive the lane and dish the ball out to Mickey on the wing b) drive the lane and pass the ball back to Jamaal at the top of the key or c) drive the lane and score himself. In any case, the priest made sure the team was ready for their roles. He also reminded the team not to call timeout. Every member of the team put their hands in the middle and chanted, "ST. MICHAEL DEFEND US!"

"We've got a dandy one here today! St. Patrick's has just taken the lead on a basket by small forward, Antonio DeShields. Here we go. There's ten seconds left. The referee tosses the ball to Mario Sanchez...10 seconds left. He's looking....looking....and he send the ball into Hector Ruiz, St. Michael's point guard. He's at the top of the key....Seven seconds... Jamaal Jordan moves up to the key for a pick and roll....Five seconds... Ruiz drives, the defenders both converge on the point guard....Three seconds left....Ruiz passes the ball out to Mickey Sullivan....He has a wide open shot....Will he get it off? Will it go in????? 'Swish!' HE HIT THE SHOT! MICKEY SULLIVAN SENDS ST.MICHAEL'S TO THE CHAMPIONSHIP GAME! WHAT AN UPSET!!!! WHAT A GAME!!!!

The players on the bench mobbed Mickey Sullivan as time expired. There was a St. Michael's team sandwich on the court. Smiles were all around as St. Michael's actually defeated the number two ranked team in the league. Father Malloy cracked a grin watching his team celebrate. How far they had they come to become true winners. Father Malloy respectfully walked over to the opposing coach and shook hands. St. Patrick's coach displayed great class as he wished Father Malloy well and he hoped that Malloy and St. Michael's would go on to win it all. Whether he meant it or not, no one could say for sure, but the respectful gesture was greatly appreciated by the priest.

Sunday, December 24, 2013

Christmas Eve! Father Malloy was so excited. He loved Christmas more than any other holiday. Father Malloy was attracted to all the holiday customs: *eggnog, Christmas carols, Ebenezer Scrooge, the eight tiny reindeer, Christmas trees, "It's a Wonderful Life", and Nativity scenes.* It was such a wonderful time of the year. This year was a very special one because of the basketball team. He told Jamaal and Hector to make sure they were all there for the Christmas Eve midnight mass.

Midnight mass was one of the most solemn and holy masses in all of Catholicism. The priest was excited to begin the festivities. One sight to behold was the plethora of Catholics attending mass. There wasn't an extra seat in the house and it wasn't only because it was Christmas Eve. The church was thriving again. Malloy was certain that the church would survive.

Father Malloy had an extra bounce in his step as he celebrated the mass. For one, it was Christmas and secondly, the basketball team had made it into the championship game. The priest was grateful for where he was in his life. The loneliness that haunted him was fading. This new mission of working with the boys of St. Michael's was the pinnacle of his career. Sure, he had met bishops and cardinals, but helping the young men of St. Michael's warmed his heart. *My cup overflows*, Malloy thought to himself.

Malloy read the Nativity story to the parishioners and he asked the members of the parish to feel grateful for all of God's gifts. Father Malloy was always moved by the following words found in the book of Matthew:

"Foxes have dens and birds have nests, but the Son of Man has no place to lay his head."

My brothers and sisters, always remember to love your neighbor. The Lord came to this world in the poorest of ways. Likewise, we need to take care of our poorer neighbors. Tiny Tim said it best. God bless us, everyone!

A rare round of applause echoed throughout the gothic-style halls. This uplifted the priest. Not that he needed any help. The priest was excited to give special Christmas gifts to his basketball players.

After the church services were over, he asked the boys to wait for him at the front pews of the church. Every player obliged as they genuflected in front of the altar and sat down quietly. "Why do you think he wants us here? It's already 1:00 in the morning," replied a tired Christopher Medina. Wanting to make sure the team took Father Malloy seriously, Jamaal replied, "Is it past your bedtime, grandpa?" The boys were all smiles as they patiently waited for their priest.

"Boys, this year has been so very special to me. You have all made such a great impact on my life. I hope you can say the same. I thought long and hard about what the perfect gift would be. And I want you to know that I've found it. And here they are."

Father Malloy looked like Santa Claus pulling small boxes out of a burgundy sack. *"I want you all to know that what I'm handing you can help you your entire life. In each of these boxes rests rosary beads. These rosary beads are different but they are also the same. The rosary prayers are always the same. Just like being a member of the team, we are all the same. It does not matter how many minutes you play, how many baskets you score, you are all equally teammates. These beads are also different. I had each one specifically sent from the origin of your family. For example, Christopher Medina, I had these rosary beads sent over from a Spanish church in Madrid.*

Christopher's' rosary beads were chiseled and carved in wood with beautiful bright blues, greens and reds.

"Pablo and Mario, these are for you two. They are from Mexico City." The two brothers smiled wide and gave the priest a hug. Father Malloy graciously embraced both young men. Malloy overjoyed to see his players appreciate the gifts.

Father Malloy continued to hand out unique rosary beads for each player. *"Mickey, here is your gift."* Father Malloy handed Sullivan Connemara marble rosary beads. Mickey Sullivan, being Irish-Catholic, realized that these rosary beads came from across the Atlantic Ocean. Mickey was well aware that Connemara marble came only from one place, his beloved Ireland. Mickey just stood there with tears welling up in his eyes. He couldn't wait to go home and show his family.

Joseph Tucker, who was Italian on his mother's side, was given rosary beads from the Vatican. *"Joseph, your gift is from the home of St. Peter and our pope. You are a coach, and there will come a time when just like the pope, you will lead this team!"* Joseph was stunned and confused at the priest's words, but he was smart enough to know that the priest was serious. Joseph solemnly rested the beads in his hands and thanked the padre with a firm handshake.

Each player on the team was given the same gift, but in a special way. They were personalized from background or purpose. The boys felt love. Each one felt special. They took great pride in knowing they were the priest's favorite sons.

Finally, there was Hector's gift. His rosary beads were sent from *The Basilica of Our Lady of Guadalupe* in Northern Mexico City, Mexico. The Mexican rosaries were carved out of wood and were beautifully hand painted. They were the grandest rosary beads the young man had ever seen. But something was different about Hector's gift. There was more to it. Inside the box, there were two envelopes folded in half.

In great wonder, Hector unfolded the envelope. Inside the envelope was money- $380.00 worth. Hector looked up at the priest, and Malloy gave him a knowing glance. Hector's eyes were wide now and he could barely breathe.

Underneath the money there was something else. The second envelope was much thinner. It was folded several times over. Hector opened the envelope and saw that inside rested a single sheet of loose-leaf paper. The paper contained a poem. Thinking this strange, Hector once again looked up at the priest. Father Malloy nodded to Hector suggesting that Hector read the poem to himself. The poem was entitled, "Hector Remember." It read as follows:

Hector Remember

Choose to do the things that are right

Help your fellow man as best you can

Always remember the lessons you've learned

Love your neighbor as yourself

I know you will be a great success

Call me if you ever need a helping hand

Eternally yours, Father Malloy

Hector was becoming emotional. No one had loved him so much as to write him a letter. He stared at the poem in wonder and appreciation. But, soon, the feeling of appreciation halted like a sudden gust of wind changing the direction of a leaf on the ground. He remembered in English class that some poems were acrostic, meaning that it spelled out a word. His eyes widened, knots were tied up in his stomach and he became nauseous.

There, before him, was his sin described in poetic form. Understanding that Hector now realized the reality of the situation, he calmly walked over to him and put his hand on his shoulder. "To error is to be human; to forgive – divine. We all make mistakes in this life. I just want to make sure you don't do anything like that ever again. I'm counting on you, Hector Ruiz!"

The tears were streaming down Hector's face and it was clear that he needed a moment. Father Malloy placed his arm on Hector's back and brought him to one of the side pews so they could talk. "Hector, do you know the story of the Prodigal Son?" Hector shook his head as he wiped his cold and now wet nose.

Once there were two brothers who inherited wealth from their living father. The first son left the town and spent all of his money on foolish things, only to become broke in a short time. The other son remained loyal to the father, working and serving the father's land. When the first son was hungry and destitute, he decided he would ask his father if he could work for him for food. Upon seeing the son, the father ran to him and embraced him warmly. He put a ring on the son's finger and ordered a feast in his honor. The first son did not think his brother deserved the warmth of the father, but he got it anyway. When the other son jealously asked why there was a party in the other son's honor when he always remained faithful, the father responded with this: "Your brother was dead and is now alive. He was lost and now is found."

...Hector, do you see? You are the Prodigal Son! You are now reborn and I know you will do great things!"

Hector fell into Malloy's arms. "I'm sorry, coach." It was obvious that Hector had turned a new leaf. "But, I can't take this

122

money, it's yours." Father Malloy pretended to take that thought into consideration and then responded, "You will take that money and everything will be settled. Now, that's an order!" Hector slowly nodded his head in agreement. The rest of the team looked on in quiet wonder. They didn't exactly know what happened, but they knew enough to stay out of it. This was between the point guard and the priest.

Unbeknownst to Father James Malloy, the players actually scrapped together some money to buy him a new fishing rod. They also game Malloy a team jersey with the name *Our Father* on the back sporting the number one. The jersey, gold and black, was signed by every player. It only meant the world to the priest.

Malloy was astonished at how much the boys grew as people. They were so much more like men today than when he had first set eyes on them. He casually walked back to the rectory where he sat himself down on a red velvet arm chair. Staring at him was the letter from the Cardinal. He knew this offer was a "once-in-a-lifetime" proposition. Moreover, refusal would be taken as an insult and secondly, it was where he always desired to work. Despite these facts, Father Malloy decided he was where he needed to be. So many times in his life, he was sent somewhere to fix, but he never considered these places home. This team, St. Michael's, meant everything to Father Malloy. Even the promise of working with Rome and the Pope himself was not enough to change his mind.

Father Malloy almost forgot to tell Hector the news. "Hector, come here! Come here, quickly!" Hector was humbled by the events of the night. He walked over to the coach with a renewed spirit. "Hector, listen, I have a friend over at Holy Family. The parish has been getting a new influx of Latino parishioners.

They need a translator. I put in a good word for your mother, Esmeralda." Hector was once again, in disbelief. *How could someone be so generous and so forgiving?* "Thank you, Father Malloy. I owe you big time."

"You do not owe me anything. Please tell your mom Merry Christmas for me."

"Ok Coach! No problem."

Chapter 14:

"There is no greater love than to lay down one's life for one's friends."

– John 15:13

Spending time with Father Malloy on Christmas Eve was eye-opening for Hector. He couldn't believe that the priest gave him the money to settle the score with Terry and the Snipers. The rest of the team and Father Malloy decided to play holiday music and watch the Knicks game that was on television.

Since it was Christmas Eve, Hector thought it was a perfect time to settle his debt with Terry. He figured Terry would be either at his home or by the school yard. It was getting dark out and it was of course, very cold. He approached the school yard and Terry was with a few of his boys. It looked as though they were drinking beers and celebrating their recent successes – however immoral as they might be. Hector became nervous. He could feel the sweat dripping off of his chest as the bubble jacket was now serving as an overly warm blanket. There was a chance that the Snipers would still go after him. However, Hector was counting on his once-solid friendship with Terry to save him. As he approached the group, The Snipers called out, "Hey, that's Hector!" Instantly, all five young men, muscular and full of hate, darted towards Hector. "I've got your money!" Hector called out in a loud voice so all could hear. Terry responded, "Yea, you betta have the money!" Hector was frightened. He asked Terry if he could speak to him privately. Terry looked back at his boys and nodded. It was only because of their history together that Terry granted his request. "Look, Terry, I didn't know that kid was in your gang. My mom really needed money

126

and I had to do what I had to do. You know what I mean?"
Terry listened with his hands folded together like the president of
a company contemplating buying or selling stock.

"I tell you what I'm gonna do for you," Terry replied in a relaxed
sort-of-way. "I'm gonna take your money, and since I've known
you for a long time, I'm going to give you a break. But, that
priest of yours is gonna pay for embarrassing me. That's for
sure." Terry snatched the money out of Hector's hands.

Hector pleaded his case to Terry with great fervor. "Don't go
after Father Malloy, Terry. He's a good guy. He's really tried to
help us. C'mon man, you don't have to do that."

"I can and I will. Now, you've pissed me off. Now, I'm going
to shoot up your entire squad! And if you want to live, you'll be
out of my sight in the next ten seconds!" Terry's eyes were wild
and Hector's stomach dropped as if he was on a never ending
rollercoaster.

Hector quickly did as he was told. He ran out of there was fast
as he could. Now, there was only one permeating thought
running back and forth in his mind. *I have to warn the priest!*
Hector knew he did not have much time now that Terry
announced his plans. Hector made a B-line for St. Michael's.
Terry and the Snipers were following Hector to St. Michael's.
Hector had to get to Malloy and the team before Terry found
them. *This is all my fault!* Hector thought to himself. With all
his might and energy, Hector made it to the church before the
gang. He looked up at the church; trying to catch his breath he
stared at the rosary beads swaying in the wind. He closed his
eyes and prayed for help. Instead of going through the side
entrance, Hector knocked at the front door. This way, Hector
figured, the team would not be alarmed.

Father Malloy opened the church doors and Hector hugged him quickly. "Father, call the police! Terry and the Snipers are coming here right now. You are in trouble and so are the guys. Terry wants to attack the entire team." No sooner than the words passed Hector's lips, Father Malloy noticed a group of teenagers turning the corner. Instantly, Father Malloy grabbed Hector and shoved him inside the church. "Call the police and take the team into the sacristy."

"I won't leave you!" Hector emphatically declared.

"That's an order! Go now! The Lord is with you and He is with me! Now, move!" Malloy then locked the church doors sealing the team in safety. Now it was Father Malloy facing the gang.

The five muscular and rugged individuals, whose ages ranged from 17 – 21 years of age, approached the church steps. Malloy had great reason to be afraid, and yet, he wasn't. He was going to protect his flock. He decided to march against the lions.

"Grab him!" The older Snipers grabbed the priest and began to hurt him. Terry, himself, punched Malloy hard in the stomach. "That's for embarrassing me!" The priest tried to defend himself, but there were too many of them. After several swings and connections, some of the Snipers became cognizant of what was occurring. They were beating down a priest, a man of the cloth. "C'mon, Terry, give it up." Some of the young teens were trying to pull Terry away, but he was merciless. Blood stained his collar as Terry pummeled his face and kicked him several times after he went to the ground.

Hector phoned the police and told the boys that Father Malloy had a message in the sacristy for them. He did not want them to know the truth for they would have been subject to attack. Hector, however, did not wait with the team. He loved the priest too much was to leave him helpless. Hector looked out the window and witnessed the vicious blows delivered by Terry. Infuriated, Hector unlocked the door and exited the church. He could not stand idly by while his mentor was in grave danger. "STOP! STOP IT RIGHT NOW! I JUST CALLED THE POLICE!" He then relocked the door and slammed it shut so no one could enter. Instantly, he jumped on top of Terry. Terry's attention then went to Hector, but sirens rang out in the streets. Two squad cars emerged and the Snipers scattered. The policemen drew their pistols and arrested five Snipers, including Terry Spinner.

Even though Hector was able to limit the blows by Terry, the damage was already done. Father Malloy, could not speak. He was unconscious. Hector was fighting back tears staring at the person who had helped him the most. Hector knew of only one thing to do, pray. He began to say the *Hail Mary* and the *Our Father* asking God to spare one of his own servants.

The E.M.T. workers tended to Father Malloy. Hector asked if he could go with the priest in the ambulance. However, since he was not family, he was not permitted to go. After the ambulance left for the hospital and after the police questioning, Hector stared out into the night. A feeling of guilt began to take over his body. He became despondent realizing that all of this was his fault. Hector knew the team was waiting for him in the sacristy. Instead of telling them, he left a note on the door telling them that Father Malloy had an emergency to tend to.

Hector was disgusted with himself. Despite his shame, he knew he had a responsibility to tell the team. He decided it would be better to call all the guys in the morning. Hector took the city bus and walked three blocks to the hospital. He wanted to stay there with the priest. The point guard made his way up to Father Malloy's room where he found Alice speaking with one of the nurses. Alice was called by the hospital as the "closest relative."

"Excuse me, but can I sit in there with Fr. Malloy?" Hector approached both Alice and the nurse in a respectful tone. "Yes, you can, but visiting hours are over in 45 minutes." Father Malloy was not awake. Hector was distraught. He had to bare his soul. The nurse and Alice could tell that Hector wanted a moment alone with Father Malloy, so they stood outside of the room.

"Father Malloy, I'm sorry. I'm so sorry. This is all my fault. If I never dealt with the gang or stole from that kid, this would never have happened. You must get better. We need you. We all need you. You mean everything to us now. Please forgive me! Please God, help Father Malloy."

Father Malloy's fingers began to move and Hector grabbed the moving hand with both of his. For the rest of the time, Hector just stared at the priest as if it were his own father on his death bed.

Alice could see the impact Father Malloy had on the basketball team. She was offered a private waiting area to stay in overnight, but instead, she offered the room to Hector. Without hesitation, Hector accepted the offer. He made himself a make-shift bed out of two chairs and a blanket. It was late and he was exhausted. He was uncomfortable, but his dreary body succumbed to natural fatigue and fell asleep. The once beautiful night turned dark and cold.

Chapter 15:

"I am a member of a team, and I rely on the team, I defer to it and sacrifice for it, because the team, not the individual, is the ultimate champion."

- Mia Hamm

"Oh my God! What happened?" Joseph Tucker was the first to arrive. "What sup' man. It was the Snipers. They went after him because of me. It's my fault. I'm going to leave the team." Hector responded in a defeated tone. Tucker could only shake his head in disappointment and agony. Even thought it was Christmas morning, the entire team slowly arrived to check on their favorite priest. Jamaal picked Mario and Pablo up in his beat up car and drove over. Mickey and Peter took the city bus together. It didn't take long before the entire team was huddled around their coach.

"Yo, guys....I have something I gotta tell you. This is all my fault. I messed up...big time. I stole money from this kid who was in the Snipers so my mom wouldn't go broke. When they found out it was me, they came after me, but Father Malloy stopped them. This was payback for helping me. Listen, I'm gonna get out of here. Just make sure the priest is taken care of."

"Hector, STOP!" yelled Jamaal. He took in a deep breath and began speaking on behalf of the team. "Listen, man, Father Malloy taught us to stick together no matter what. He taught us to trust each other, to care about each other. We aren't gonna turn our back on you. You're our brother."

Hector was encouraged by those words, but they weren't enough. He continued to the door. Henry Patterson stepped in front of him and put his hand on Hector's shoulder. "You're not going anywhere! You're our point guard and you're part of this team whether you like it or not." Then, each player chimed in with their own reason or statement to push the point guard to stay. Hector was touched, but still, it was not enough. That is, it wasn't enough until a scratched and raspy voice echoed in the cramped vanilla-colored room.

"Heecctor!" Father Malloy's volume was so low you had to stick your neck out to him in order to better hear him. "You....are my son. You are all my sons. I need you to remember everything that I've taught you, no matter what happens to me."

"You're not going anywhere!" Mario declared. "And we're going to cancel the championship game."

"YOU WILL NOT!" Father Malloy's eyes seemed to pop out of his face and his hands turned to fists. "We worked all this time to reach this point. You are all going to play this game and you're going to win. I know it!"

Jamaal interjected, "But, Father Malloy, who would coach us?"

"That's easy." Father Malloy put his hand by his neck. He was having trouble speaking. "Joseph will coach."

Joseph Tucker swallowed hard. He had loved being Malloy's assistant all year. But to coach the championship game was surely beyond his abilities.

"I know what you're thinking, Joseph. But, you can do it! You've been studying and scouting all year. If anyone can do it, you can."

The other teammates began clapping and patting Joseph on the back. They had faith in him, just like his coach.

"KNOCK, KNOCK!" A short, squat man with glasses and a receding hairline entered wearing a white coat and sporting a tie and a stethoscope. "Good morning, my name is Dr. Gino Profera. I'm guessing you're members of Father Malloy's parish." "Yes, we are, and we're his players!" proudly declared Mickey.

"Well, he really should get rest. We still do not have conclusive tests done."

The doctor seemed annoyed at the large amount of people in the visiting room. He was quick to leave. Hector ran to the doctor to find out the cleric's prognosis. "He's ok, right Doc?"

"I can't really comment to non family members." The doctor was reading a chart and started to walk away.

"Please, Doc, listen to me. He's a priest. He has no family except for us. Please tell me, he's gonna be alright right?" Hector pleaded his case fearing the next words that would come out of the physician's mouth.

"There's internal bleeding. It's a 50/50 proposition." The doctor patted Hector on the arm and left.

Hector fell to his knees.

It was Christmas morning and Father Malloy needed a miracle.

The entire day, members of St. Michael's came to visit the priest. Unfortunately, they were refused. Father Malloy needed intense care. The team was asked to leave, but before they left, the priest imparted one last message.

"Remember, you're a family. You all are different, but you are all the same. We care about each other and we trust each other. When you go on that court, I'll be with you. Have faith in each other!"

With that, the team left anguished a defeated. They yearned for yesterday.

Jamaal knew the team was feeling somber and down. There was no way they were going to match the intensity necessary to compete in a championship game, let alone against mighty Our Lady of Pity. Therefore, the muscular forward asked the entire team to meet him at St. Michael's one hour before the game. They would travel together as one. The team honored Jamaal's request and they entered the church together. In silence, the team made a single file line and proceeded to walk toward the altar. Each player stopped at the first pew, genuflected in prayer and sat down. Then, Jamaal asked the team to pray for Father Malloy. "Let's say a prayer for our coach, Father Malloy."

They began to pray the prayer Father Malloy taught them.

> *Saint Michael the Archangel,*
> *defend us in battle.*
> *Be our protection against the wickedness and*
> *snares of the devil.*
>
> *Amen.*

It was a brief moment, but a powerful one. They now were reminded of the power of faith and the power of working together. It was time to complete their journey as a team.

Together, as one, they made their way to the championship court.

Saturday:

Catholic Youth Organization Championship Game

OUR LADY OF PITY vs. ST. MICHAEL'S

Two gentlemen with microphones in hand were walking back and forth to each team looking for research on the players for their broadcast. The Catholic Youth Organization Championship game would be broadcast over the radio and broadcast on the local Staten Island cable network. It was as prestigious a game as any of the players would ever participate. As a matter of fact, this would mark the end of many basketball careers. Sure, the boys might go on to play intramurals and some could perhaps play for their college. But, in the C.Y.O. league, it was the end of the line.

Joseph Tucker was holding his clipboard. He decided to dress as the coach wearing khaki pants, a yellow polo shirt and black sneakers. He had a sharpened pencil resting behind his right ear. His nerves were showing in his pacing and biting of fingernails. It was his job to navigate St. Michael's through the championship game. Every so often he would simply close his eyes and rely on the mental image of Father Malloy uttering the words, "Trust the game plan and trust in each other." Those words kept repeating themselves in his mind.

The boys were warming up for the game each in their own way. Mickey Sullivan's warm up, though was a little peculiar. As Jamaal was reaching for his toes in order to stretch out his hamstrings, Mickey took out a bottle of holy water, opened it, and began flicking the blessed liquid at Jamaal. "Hey man, what are you doing?" Jamaal wiped the water from his cheek. "Don't worry it's good for you!" Mickey replied. Seeing this, the other boys started to make eye contact with each other and began to smile. This seemed to break the tension. Mickey resembled a priest during a high mass, as the boys emphatically accepted a spraying of holy water. "Where did you get that?" Henry asked. "Father gave it to me. He said to use it for important moments. Nothing can stop us now!"

The boys, seemingly with God on their side, began to huddle around their new coach.

Radio Announcer:

Today is the day! It is the C.Y.O. championship! Our Lady of Pity and St. Michael's will be playing for it all! We'll be right back with the opening tip off!

Meanwhile…

Alice went to visit Father Malloy. She brought him chicken soup and a small radio. Hector called Alice and told her that it was extremely important to bring the radio for he knew that the game would be on the air. When Alice entered the visiting quarters, she winced at the sight of the friar. Malloy could barely see anything; his left eye was bloody and it was too swollen to fully open. Despite his unfortunate state, he was able to graciously ask Alice to turn the dial to the S.I.S. radio station. Alice fiddled with the static stations until she reached the Staten Island Sound station. When Malloy heard the correct station, he motioned to Alice with an extended palm. It was clear that Malloy wanted to listen to the game on the radio. Malloy preferred the radio over television because radio announcers were more descriptive. Besides, in Malloy's current state, a television would leave him in the dark.

*Our Lady of Pity Parish Gymnasium…

Joseph Tucker gathered the team around him. His message was simple. "We know what we have to do! If we believe we can do it, we will! Let's do this for Fr. Malloy!" The team clapped their hands in unison and Tucker sent out the starters.

Tucker sent out Father Malloy's top five:

Hector Ruiz – point guard

Mickey Sullivan – shooting guard

Christopher Medina – small forward

Jamaal Jordan – power forward

138

Now David did defeat Goliath with a rock, but when it comes to basketball, the Goliaths typically overwhelm the Davids with size and power. And in this case, Goliath was Lance Thompson. Thompson won the M.V.P. (Most Valuable Player) award for the league. He averaged 29 points per game and 10 rebounds with six assists. He even received three full scholarships to local colleges in the area. He was a nightmare for every opposing defense. The last time St. Michael's faced Our Lady of Pity, Lance Thompson destroyed Malloy's exterior and interior defense. Christopher Medina, the defensive specialist, had been thinking about this match up for weeks. He was hoping and praying for one last chance to show Thompson that he couldn't get the best of him.

Radio Announcer: "And here's the tipoff!"

Henry Patterson won the tip off and the championship game was underway. On the first possession, Hector set up a pick and roll with Jamaal, but then found a back-door-cutting Christopher Medina for a score.

On the ensuing possession, Lance Thompson drove the lane and hit a pull up 12-footer. Tucker twisted his neck in annoyance as he was hoping Thompson would start out cold. That was not to be.

Hector then brought the ball up and this time, he drove past his defender. He dished the ball to an open Jamaal Jordan who banked one home off of the glass. Our Lady of Pity again responded with a three pointer from their shooting guard, Ishmael Reynolds. Back and forth they went. Both teams knew exactly what was on the line with neither relenting.

The starting five were playing hard and playing well, but they were tiring. Medina was expending a great amount of energy covering Thompson, and he needed to sit. Tucker sent in Mario Sanchez, who provided a better long range shot. Tucker also substituted Peter Thomas for Henry Patterson, relying on the quick and smaller lineup.

This lineup was also productive. Peter and Hector were able to steal the ball one time each and get easy scores. However, this lineup revealed a great weakness. Our Lady of Pity was grabbing every offensive rebound and scoring on second chances. St. Michael's fell behind by seven going into the half.

Meanwhile…

Though in terrible physical condition, Father Malloy was acutely listening to the radio broadcast. Every time Our Lady of Pity would score, Malloy would clench his fist and pound the bed. The nurses would check in on the cleric and attempted to turn off the radio to no avail. "I need to listen. These are my boys, playing!" Malloy had no time for interruptions. "The next nurse who interrupts this priest will have to say three Hail Mary's and a Glory Be!"

Alice was no longer with Malloy as she had to go back to the parish in order to greet the visiting priest who was to celebrate the Saturday evening mass. To Alice's astonishment, the parish was filled with parishioners. All the pews were filled with people praying for Father James Malloy. Jamaal had posted the unfortunate news on the parish's website and asked for everyone's help. *If only Father Malloy could see this miracle!* Alice thought to herself. She was touched by the love people had for the relatively new priest. *One man can make a difference* she whispered to herself proudly.

Meanwhile…

"Peter Thomas gets a great pick from Henry Patterson, he curls around the pick, and fires!.....The shot is good! St. Michael's is down by five!"

There was 8:40 seconds left in the third quarter. St. Michael's was hanging in the game. At this juncture in the previous meeting, St. Michael's had been down by double-digits. This time, however, their familiarity and continuity paid dividends. The players were lighter on their feet, swiftly skimming their legs off the floor of the court. They were honoring their defensive assignments, trusting in each other. They were running their offensive plays with pin-point precision. The only smudge on the masterpiece was the difference in pure athleticism. Our Lady of Pity had so much fire power. Their players were hitting intermediate and three-point shots with great regularity. Even the shots that were missed were then gobbled up by their strong front line. St. Michael's couldn't get enough stops. Tucker had to call timeout. Tucker knew if he didn't try something different, the result would be the same as the last time they met. In Tucker's heart of hearts, there was no room for moral victories. St. Michael's had to win this game.

"We need to take some chances on defense! I'm going to make a change. We're going to a zone, but this time, I want Christopher up top on the guards. I'm also moving Jamaal to small forward. I want a bigger man on their best player. Now, let's get some stops!"

This was an unorthodox move because Jamaal had not played small forward all year. It was a gamble, but in Tucker's mind, they were destined to lose if he did absolutely nothing.

Our Lady of Pity inbounded the ball; Hector and Christopher were like black mamba snakes striking hard at the opposing guards. They caused a turnover right away, which led to a Mickey Sullivan eight-foot-jumper. On the ensuing possession, Thompson seemed bothered by Jamaal's size. He could not get around him as easily as the smaller players. Thompson relied on his speed to blow by Jamaal, but Patterson came over from the weak side and altered his shot. Finally, St. Michael's earned a stop. This newfound energy and vivacious defense brought St. Michael's back. They tied to game going into the fourth quarter.

Meanwhile…

Lying helpless on the hospital bed, Father Malloy asked the nurse to fetch his black jacket. Inside the pocket were a set of rosary beads. Malloy started praying for his players.

The fourth quarter resembled a Roman gladiator match. Both teams wanted the win, each team hitting huge shots. Every player in both uniforms did everything they could to help their team win the game. The players for St. Michael's were courageous in battle. Hector dished and dashed, Mickey stopped and popped, Christopher swiped and swatted, Patterson tipped balls in and Jamaal pivoted and poured in with precious precision. St. Michael's was playing their guts out.

"60 seconds left! It's a shame one of these teams has to lose." The new coach, Joseph Tucker, called a time out. He designed a play where Patterson and Jamaal would set a pick for both Christopher and Mickey. The play worked to perfection as Hector found an open Christopher Medina. Two players converged on him and he dropped the ball down low to an open Jamaal Jordan for the go ahead score! Jamaal was so excited; he came over to Tucker and gave him a giant bear hug. They were actually in the lead 72-71. But there was still time on the clock.

Radio Announcer:

"Twenty seconds left! Our Lady of Pity has the ball down one. This could be the last play of the game. The referee hands the ball to the power forward, Rich Brewer. Brewer passes the ball to Lance Thompson. It's Thompson bringing the ball up to the top of the key. He's staring into Hector Ruiz's eyes, dribbling....he fakes left....now he fakes right....He drives the lane! Ruiz is sticking with him...Jamaal Jordan steps up...THOMPSON STOPS! POPS!............And SCORES!!!!!!!!!!!!!!!!!HE HIT IT!!!! WHAT A SHOT!!!! OUR LADY OF PITY TAKES THE LEAD!!!!!

ST. MICHAEL'S CALLS A TIME OUT WITH ONLY FIVE SECONDS REMAINING ON THE CLOCK!

"What a game folks! What a game! The championship hangs in the balance. Our Lady of Pity is clinging to a one point lead with just five seconds left on the clock. St. Michael's has one last shot to win the championship!"

Hector Ruiz was emotionally spent. He had been waiting for this limelight moment for years. To his amazement, all he could think about at this point were others. These thoughts revolved around his tired mother and his loving coach. Tears welled up in Hector's eyes. He knew he had to pull himself together. It all came down to one play – one play for the championship. Hector knew his team and his coach were counting on him.

Then, he did something unexpected. He called time out.

With his teammates all looking at him, he frantically ran over to the bench and motioned for the entire team to quickly huddle together. They looked more like a football team, with Hector as the quarterback on one knee. This was Hector's moment, but he knew it was really all about someone else.

"We all know we have to win this game for Father Malloy. He has done so much for all of us. If it weren't for him, my life would be in shambles. Everyone get your rosary beads out, lift them in the air, and pray for the priest!"

As quickly as they could, each young man dug Father Malloy's Christmas gifts out of their duffle bags. With rosary beads in hand, they all said one Hail Mary, together as one.

Hail Mary, full of grace....The Lord is with Thee...Blessed art thou amongst women and blessed is the fruit of Thy womb Jesus.

144

Holy Mary, Mother of God, pray for us sinners, now and at the hour of our death. Amen.

The teammates were now one entity with one specific goal inspired by one man of dignity and faith.

"St. Michael!" Hector shouted.

"PRAY FOR US!" the rest of the team chanted in unison.

The boys proudly stood together and continued to elevate their rosaries into the air. All of a sudden, the players seemed to forget about their own problems. They were all thinking about their coach. Hector decided to wrap the rosary beads around his wrist. Win or lose, Hector was going to go out on that court with his coach and his faith.

Meanwhile...

Father Malloy was silently lying in his hospital bed with his neck turned to the left, where the radio was resting. The good priest was listening attentively to the radio call. In agony, the priest made the sign of the cross with his right hand. He ran the rosary beads through his fingers. He wrapped them around his hands and joined the boys in prayer. Though miles apart, they were united. They would all face the lions together.

"And it appears as if the St. Michael's basketball team is huddling up before the final play. And I think the players are each holding something in their hands. It's hard to tell from our angle, but their leading scorer, Hector Ruiz, is on one knee. Whatever is being said, this team is demonstrating great unity and sportsmanship in the face of adversity. The absent coach, Fr. James Malloy, would be proud of his team today....

After the prayer, Joseph Tucker diagramed a play that would utilize Hector's speed. Jamaal Jordan would set a pick for Hector and he would go to the hole as quickly as possible. Everyone had lumps in their throats, but not Hector.

...Here they come. St. Michael's has the ball with five seconds to play. They will inbound the ball at half-court. Mickey Sullivan is the in-bounder. Our Lady of Pity is in a man-to-man defense. Here we go! The referee hands the ball to Sullivan. Mickey Sullivan is looking for a player, looking for a player. He better get it in before the five seconds expire. He passes the ball to Ruiz at the top of the key. FOUR SECONDS LEFT!!!! HECTOR RUIZ DRIVES HARD INTO THE PAINT...TWO SECONDS LEFT...HE PULLS UP AT THE FOUL LINE...HERE'S THE FINAL SHOT...AND THE SHOT IS......."

While the last play was set in motion, Father Malloy fell into a deep sleep. Whether or not the shot went in was of no consequence. Father Malloy's team had already attained victory. His boys were playing together, praying together, living together as a family. He was incredibly proud. It was one of the most fulfilling moments of his life. With true victory in hand, the priest's mission was complete. The loneliness he once felt was now gone for eternity. Father Malloy and his boys faced the lions and won.

THE END.

My Favorite Priests – Real and Fictional

Monsignor Philip Franceschini

*Monsignor always made us feel proud to be altar boys. He would routinely remark that we were the best in the city. Whether that was true or not was not important, what was important was that those words made us feel special.

Father David Kosmoski

*He barely knew my wife and me upon moving to New Jersey, and yet, he graciously agreed to marry us. He also blessed my brother's motorcycle! He is truly a Renaissance man as he is an accomplished painter, teacher, landscaper, and carpenter. He does the work of five men. He is everything a priest should be.

Father Kevin Creagh

*Wonderful priest for the young adults in America. I remember on September 11, 2001, Father Kevin helped so many students at St. John's University cope with that tragic day. He is a brilliant educator and an excellent writer. Father Kevin wrote the most eloquent recommendation letter that I've ever received. Along with his brilliance, he is also down to earth. Once he listened to my confession wearing a Nike shirt. I thought that was cool.

Father John Mercer

*Worked with Father Mercer at Our Lady of Pity as a teacher's assistant for C.C.D. I'll never forget when he requested my mother's famous Irish soda bread while giving his homily. Our mouths hit the floor.

Father Chuck O'Malley

"Going My Way" –

Father O'Malley, played by Bing Crosby, had charm, good looks, and was clever. He also could sing like no other. He was a do-it-all guy who seemed to make everything better without taking any credit himself. I sing "Too-Ra-Loo-La-Lu-La" to my daughter all the time.

The Whisky Priest-

The Power and the Glory

In Graham Greene's novel, The Power and the Glory, the whiskey priest is a sinner and a hypocrite. Despite his human weakness, he finds the courage to face the atheistic and wretched Red Shirts. His sacrifice is one that made me proud to be Catholic.

ABOUT THE AUTHOR

Ryan Murphy was born and raised in Staten Island, New York. Currently, he works as an English teacher at an intermediate school in Staten Island, New York. He resides in New Jersey with his wife and daughter.